The Gentle Art
Of Sanity

Louise M. Hart

chipmunkapublishing
the mental health publisher

Published by
Chipmunkapublishing

http://www.chipmunkapublishing.com

Copyright © Louise M. Hart 2013

ISBN 978-1-84991-955-5

Chipmunkapublishing gratefully acknowledge the support of Arts Council England.

Biography of Louise M. Hart

Louise M. Hart was born in Northumberland in 1968. At the age of three, her parents' marriage broke down and she moved with her Mother to Coventry. Her school years were fraught with difficulties, never quite, "fitting in" she was perceived by staff and other students as somewhat quiet and introspective. During this time, she discovered a facility for creative writing, providing an escape from the torment of the life experience.

However, against the odds, she was awarded a place at the University of North London in 1990, where she studied a degree in English and philosophy. This was to be the best and the worst time of her life. Louise became a central figure at her college campus and a keen political activist, but behind the mask, her concept of self was crumbling and her vision of reality challenged.

In 1993, overwhelmed by paranoia and depression, she was diagnosed with psychosis and quit her university course just a few months before it was due to be completed. She spent the next few years as a revolving door patient of the local psychiatric hospital. Frequent medication changes and social isolation only heightened her despair.

Having experienced a hypermanic episode in 2002, Louise was subsequently diagnosed with bipolar disorder, which, is, now, controlled, by a maintenance dose of medication and a variety of coping strategies, informed by her experiences.

Her almost lifelong ambition to become a published writer became realised when she, finally, summoned the courage to submit work to a publisher. Now, living in Largs, in Scotland, she writes both poetry and prose, and recently, has begun to write a second novel. She hopes that during her lifetime, she will experience not only a change in social attitudes towards mental ill health, but improvements in the care and treatment of clients with mental health problems by and those who work within the system.

CHAPTER ONE

Cat-Hater decided that he was alive, for he had survived the toil of a night, whose imagery had blinded him to the certainty of the impending day. He awoke on the stroke of seven, his alarm clock reminding him that he was, now, a worker employed to engage with a wage packet at the end of each month. He bade his bed a thankful farewell and rediscovered the joy of the first bathroom break of the day. Rinsing his face in cold water, he looked in the mirror.

More beast than man, his reflection snarled back. Eyes rejected by the sockets in which they usually resided hung, like roses, red and dying. His skin had the expression of cellophane. Like a room whose door had always been locked, his foundations prohibited him from accessing the creature behind the glass; the mirror remained intact. Drowning it in suds of shaving foam, he erased its bestial features. Tears rushed down his face like sprinters reaching the final furlong; he wanted to walk until the dread had left him, so he walked around his flat. Briefly, he remembered the unopened bottles of tablets in his bathroom cabinet and almost smiled.

Although devoid of physical pain, he knew that torment had occupied his stomach. He managed to dress and headed for work. Observing the world through a window of a bus, the city of the blind rolled before his eyes. His ipod played a familiar tune, "Breathe, breathe in the air. Don't be afraid to care." Reaching into his bag, he pulled out the book he had read three times that week; it was Tuesday. Devouring every syllable, he thawed in the heat of the first sentence,

"Horselover Fat's nervous breakdown began the day he got the phone call from Gloria." Every time a thought did not derive from his head and threatened to inform his consciousness, he fought to focus on the novel. For words between his ears fed his fears like an image of bloodied tears within the eye of his mind. The words in the novel reminded him how well he was now that he had experienced the unseen. On the culmination of his journey, Cat-Hater thrust his book into his bag, turned off his ipod and stepped off the bus. His workplace towered above him like a gluttonous monster anticipating its first meal

of the day. As usual, Cat-Hater's stomach burned with acid dread. He closed his mind and shut down his heart. He wanted to run away, but his legs crawled on. A four-minute walk to doom loomed on the horizon; the horizon glistened black and old.

Inwardly, he pleaded not to be asked to work in room four. The room in which the one whom he abhorred reigned furiously over her compliant charges. Thus, he smiled ironically when he read the list of staff names assigned to each room and saw the number four above his own. The defeated man slunk down the corridor and entered into his uncertain fate.

She had already arrived. She, his co-worker, with eyes of iron and a soul of shit. "D'ya wanna cup of tea?" How many times had he told her that he only drank coffee?

"It's okay. I'll make myself a coffee," he replied, knowing that were she to make his drink it would taste more like piss and washing-up liquid than caffeine.

"Let's have a fag." Her words came later. Pretending that he did not hate her, he sat with her in the smoker's hut avoiding a crescendo of questions euphemistically portraying curiosity. "Are you married?"

"No. I lived with a woman once. For four weeks. But, she kicked me out because I changed my knickers everyday and always put the toilet seat down."

Between nine and nine thirty a.m. the service users entered room four. Kev was so profoundly autistic that a misplaced chair could prompt an aggressive reaction. He roared like a lion and was as vulnerable as a lamb. Because she shone like the sun, Tim had flashed a knife at his Mother; she had phoned the police. And Mary Jane, who had the face of a distorted angel, shook in expectation of the bullying hands of those around her, unable to verbalise her pain.

Cat-Hater sat beside Ram, whose words bound his throat and strangled like rope. Choking on his saliva, his only utterances were semi-formed coughs. Cat-Hater reached into the mind of his companion and pulled out a screaming hole. So moved was he by the texture of his discovery that he laughed until he shed tears. "What's the joke?" said soul of shit.

"I'll take Ram for a walk in the garden." He spluttered; his head buried in his chest to disguise the laughter buried in his raspberry face.

A kick up the arse (his), tongues (theirs) choking on tablets prescribed by rich/witch doctors attempting to silence the silent, a fix of nicotine to punctuate his life sentence and another workday had ended. The evaporation of a few hours in the whole scheme of the venture released his psyche from the monotony of fate. Cat-Hater cast away his sword and climbed home.

Daily rituals continued. The hell's hole of work drilled into his being, reawakening feelings of inconsequentiality. For Cat-Hater Slim, the most productive hour of the day lay between two and three a.m. when he would drown his soul in a haze of smoke and vodka. Reclining to the stereophonic tinkle of sounds from a bygone age, he possessed the face of an infant, but the mind of a sage. Then he picked up a pen.

The simple ballpoint pen glistened sapphire blue, he embraced its waist and listened to the thoughts it brought forth surfaced in ink. Cat-Hater became a worker of words, a boss in his true workplace, the desk and the chair. The pen became a life force permitting him air. Energy flowed from the pen, into his hand and culminated in an explosion of belief about the premeditated nature of his writing. It is my destiny to mould the words, but something lies behind their strokes and curves.

Cat-Hater had considered a pill, but accepted the pen. Never again, will I fall beneath the wheels of sickness; my mental quickness will never be retarded by the imbalance of a tablet. And the words poured from the tip of his pen onto paper.

Approximately 2.17 on Thursday morning. Cat-Hater inhaled his spliff as if it was the last taste of cancer he would ever experience. "Take me to truth," his mind bellowed. Sweet droplets of sweat pierced his face; his heart pounded to the beat of an anxiety so deeply hidden that it penetrated even the forbidden parts of his soma, hidden by his pyjamas. His body ascended with increasing speed, like a rocket with limitless suspension, into an opaque atmosphere free of all illustration. His mind, like his vision, became nothingness. His ego, denigrated beneath his shoes, scrambled for attention. The return trip was less fun.

Back on earth, Cat-Hater's inner vision became externalised in a cinematic tribute to his life. The film filled his eyes with tears, bulbously revealed and clouding his sight with memories of years best forgotten. Clinging to his Mother's womb, he resisted the force of her birth canal. An instrument of torture sought him, pulled flesh against flesh. His Mother's wound became his own and the screech of life pounded his chest until he experienced the agony of a first breath. By the age of two, his insomnia had transformed into hypomania. His fascination with electricity reflected a death wish, which had been prohibited from being realised by the abortive eyes and quick responses of his Mother. Fuck you Mother.

When he reached the age of ten his sentence had begun. Pissing against walls with Cousin Dave lead to his first denigration. He had always felt uncomfortable about their age difference; Dave was nineteen when he first showed Cat-Hater the full extent of his manhood. Cat-Hater hoped that when he grew up his dicky would not be as ugly and smelly as that of his cousin. He experienced nightmares whose content, over time, became increasing synonymous with his lived experience. He remembered his Mother, pride heaving violently with every movement of her cumulous breasts, pressing her hand into his hand into his groin. "My boy's very big," she had boasted before a small ensemble of female friends. "Certainly doesn't get it from his Father." Cat-Hater fell to his knees and prayed for redemption.

The morning after the night before began with a sore head and the stench of urine in his bed. He telephoned work and said that he had been up all night with diarrhoea. "Good shit," he thought, opening a can of larger. He eyed-up his copy of the Bible and when he looked inside and found an old, forgotten photo, torn from a porn magazine tears christened his eyes. He put the photo in his pocket and with the sacrificial flame of his cigarette lighter burned the Bible. Momentarily, he fancied that he saw a face in the flames, then he blinked his eyes and saw only red.

Friday night was his night out with his comrades; members of the Revolutionary Socialist Party who sat behind their half-pints of larger attempting to right the wrongs of a world to which Cat-Hater did not belong. But, invariably, he was the first person to arrive, done up like the dog's bollocks and pretending to be alive. He slipped into the chair nearest to the bar and downed his first pint in ten minutes. When Vlad entered the pub, Cat-Hater suppressed his desire to prostrate himself in tribute to his branch's only paid full-time organiser and walked outside where he lit a fire at the end of his oral protrusion. Che looked very fetching, that night, dressed from head to toe in army surplus gear and pretending not to be gay.

Even when suggesting that comradely weight was not being pulled, Rosa occupied her throne like serenity's queen. Cat-Hater knew that his wrist had been slapped. For it limped to the right and turned a delicate shade of blue. Scowling beneath his frown, Cat-Hater rose to his feet and croaked,

"Would you like to hear my poem?" Greeted by a uniform snigger of silence, his vocal chords wobbled like a twelve year old after a couple of vodkas, a pint of Guinness and a bottle of wine, but the rhymes of his tongue sounded wrong to everyone, but himself.

"They said that I was psychotic

They said, "You're very ill."

They gave me orange syrup and too many happy pills.

The doctor was against me

She put thoughts into my mind

She ought to be punished

Mental rape is a crime.

Ostensibly, I am much better, now.

They say that I look very well.

But no one sees beyond my smile

The life that is lived in hell

Or the thoughts

Which drag me

Like serpents

Into pity's pit.

No one

That is

But me

Who is all mind and nearly sick.

Cat-Hater paused. He screeched, "If I am not part of the cure. I am the cause."

Che beckoned him to be seated. "What do you think of the IRA?" He asked, enthusiasm straining form every line on his unmarked face. "Do you agree with me that Gerry Adams sold them out?"

"I wish I was dead."

"They could have brought down the state." Che continued.

"I wish I was dead." Cat-Hater continued.

For Cat-Hater, work had become a blinding curse. I was made to be a writer, not a support worker. The only spirit he encountered in the gloom of the day-centre, where he worked, lay within those secret dissenters whose rebelliousness had been exhibited in behaviour labelled inappropriate. He would be their saviour, but first he had to save himself. Engaged in a flurry of thought about how he, Cat-Hater Slim, could possibly re-ignite the extinguished lights of his learning disabled service users, he sipped his cup of piss and washing up liquid and decided that he would seek respite accompanying Ram for a walk in the garden. The garden, comprising pointless concrete and stubborn attempts at flowerbeds, beckoned to him through the windows of room four. The possibility of inhaling the Spring chill, rather than the stench of shit stained nappies which other support assistants had neglected to change, prickled his skin like cacti. He had spent his half-hour dinner break crying in a corner before a trio of service users; he was not entitled to another break.

Cat-Hater had internalised Ram's behaviour codes and believed that he understood the language of his silence. "He did that choking thing again," he pleaded to soul of shit. "It might help if I took him for a walk for five minutes." Ram responded by choking even more loudly, his grey sweatshirt weighted to his chest with his sporadically flowing fountain of spittle.

"Don't be long, then," replied the one whose eyelids flickered towards the sky. "He's been a right bastard recently."

Eager to escape, Cat-Hater grabbed his bait by his wheelchair handles and proceeded to the outer. The moment his feet struck concrete, he was intercepted by light. Fluorescent green gleamed from the pores of the world; he had become the light of the dark. He enjoyed standing out. Buzzing like a cornered bee, his being bore into the concrete until they functioned as one. His limbs burned above the carpet of leaves chatting beneath his feet. Cat-Hater dumped Ram beside a stinking bin and glided over nature's decay. He collected samples of different leaves and tried to form them into a necklace, but decided to wear them as a crown instead.

"Bow down to your Queen," he beamed at Ram who, without a coat on a cold day, had begun to shiver like life deceased. With each passing second Cat-Hater advanced further up the perceptual ladder. Yellow leaves became precious gems and the mud squeezed blades of grass with orgiastic passion before dying under the weight of a clumsy foot. "I love life," Cat-Hater enthused. "What do you love? I'd give you a blow job, if it wasn't abusive." Cat-Hater noted a hint of disappointment on Ram's face. "You're a mental giant. You don't pull our hair or spit at us. You're the one for me, Rammy."

"O the sun shone bright on Mrs Porter and on her daughter they wash their feet in soda water." Spoke the non-verbal man. Cat-hater's skin nearly abandoned his body. He stared at Ram whose face portrayed nothing, but saliva. Cat-Hater had witnessed a miracle and momentarily wished that he had not burned that bible after all. Should I speak to the papers, phone the television news; social services would not approve. He grabbed Ram by his shoulders and shrieked, "Come on, talk, talk to me again." But, despite much prompting and the occasional prod, Ram was not forthcoming. Present in Cat-Hater's mind were one thousand and twenty one explanations for

Ram's verbal tease. Until, frustrated by Ram's subsequent return to silence, he decided to keep the secret to himself and returned to room four.

Upon his return, soul of shit, who until four months ago had worked in the day centre kitchen, looked down her nose and snapped, "late again." Stomach churning in a coil of adrenaline, Cat-Hater snapped back.

"Late again. Who gives a fuck? If you got out more, maybe you'd be more interested in the people around you than your watch." She marched towards him and stabbed him in the chest with the point of a finger; he interrupted her screeches by shouting as loudly as his lungs would allow, "Fuck you and fuck the job." Cat-Hater grabbed his coat and his bag and marched out of the room, the building and the lives of some service users for whom he represented the only spark in a fire of iron fuel.

In the evening Cat-Hater unwound to the sound of the screeching preacher, James Hetfield, "this search goes on." The ticking clock inside his skull made him feel ill, but he knew that it was only because he was too well. "My lifestyle determines my death style." He head butted a cushion, wrote a poem about the space between the books on his bookshelf and felt much better.

As he began to write his next poem, his telephone rang. He jumped like a cat afraid of his own reflection, as though the possibility of another threatened his subjectivity and simultaneously reminded him that he was alone.

"Hello."

A voice followed, unfamiliar and low, "hello Cat."

"Hello."

"Hello Cat." Repetition with nowhere to go.

"Who is it?" Is this someone's idea of a trick, a joke to make me sick?

"Hello Cat." Pause. The click of a telephone receiver being replaced.

As the evening unfolded, in the continuum of the night, Cat-Hater's belief about the identity of his caller evolved from that of an enemy to an executioner, for he, Cat-Hater Slim had been targeted for reciting his poem in a pub, getting pissed and mentioning death. Maybe they, also, knew about the weed. But, who were they?

They think they know me, they don't. But, I know them. I will not let them creep inside my head. Henceforth, I shall stay away from those who prey on idealists searching for something to say. My thoughts cannot be extracted; they are cushioned by beams of light, which reach to heaven out of sight of their ideological hold. Their ideologies are plated in gold, but distorted into plastic by those bought and sold on politics and wearing sloppy, knicker elastic. And their politics are exemplified by the power they desire, but claim to despise. There is no portal into my mind; they misconstrued me as the unthinking kind, but I can think right through them and their fascist smiles.

Could I be wrong, maybe it was not them on the phone. My mind could be acting as a playful imp, generating thoughts, which I do not think. After all, they are not all bad. Che is good, I think. Otherwise, why would I give him my heart? At least they have belief. I, myself, merely think I think. I own no thought being thinking's thief. The toss and turn of thought led Cat-Hater to seek refuge in late night TV. His failure to ingest the audible numbness projected by the television screen prompted him to silence the dialogue and tune into a different sound, the sound of the ticking. When the hands of his internal clock face met, he lit a cigarette and considered the spectrum of coping strategies, but could not reach beyond the first.

Experiencing the fleshy scorch of a lit cigarette against his upper arm, he whimpered from the back of his throat like a dog bound with rope. Within seconds, the pain had subsided into a steady hum of discomfort, which counteracted his internal terror. Four minutes after withdrawing the cigarette, the terror had returned. Thus, he repeated the procedure, only stopping when he had completed an image in the shape of a holy cross. Having observed the slightly jagged delineation of the vertical line, Cat-Hater tried to suppress his sense of disappointment and feeling rawer than sore mounted his bed and slept.

In his slumber, Cat-Hater was driven underground into a tunnel through which he sped in search of light. However, the darkness darted faster than his eyes could access, his vision carrying him further into its howling starkness. Falling into a precipice was not good for his health. His heart thrashed like claps of thunder and his head throbbed as though it were accessing all the wonders of the world in a simultaneous flow of neural activity. As suddenly as the darkness had come followed a festival of brightness. Shades of Technicolor splashed across Cat-Hater's retinas like the paintings of Van Gogh. The colours were shaped like animals, wild beasts of the forest and the woods. His visual field split into a million fields, each one containing creatures. He saw every feature of their beings; he saw more than he had ever seen before and it hurt so much that it felt good. He tried to open his eyes, and then he realised that they were already open.

Louise M. Hart

CHAPTER TWO

For Cat-Hater Slim time no longer existed. Spaced out in the cell, in which he dwelt, where no one could corrupt him into not being, he fed on hash cake and wrote. His poetry would touch the heart of humanity; he would stab the backs of his objectors, take arms against the professors who awarded him a mere second-class degree for three years, which nearly robbed him of his sanity.

Writing grabs me like a smile of elation whose lips I grip with the fury of nature. But, upon reading the fruits of my ventures, I am brought down by common sense. For, will anybody read this lowly verse before I am carried away in a hearse? With every stroke of my pen, death grows nearer; that which I once yielded is, now, the object of my fear. Thus, Cat-Hater's love of the pen became the purpose of his existence. He wrote into tomorrow as if today would deprive him of his last breath. It is better to express my life than die voiceless.

He had no choice, but to neglect his housework and physical appearance; writing took precedence over such trivialities. He had not ventured outside for four days or spoken to anyone outside his head. His poetry massaged his mind, but knotted his body like sticky toffee. He was rotting, but it was worth it for his art. Rarely did he sleep, until broken by exhaustion and anxiety he experienced fitful bursts of dream-fuelled visions of books whose texts were just out of sight. Every time he awoke, he became seized by a sense of frustration at being unable to read the books. He was sure that their contents were all his own work. One day he would reside in the literary canon, proving to the world that he deserved to be heard.

On the fifth day, Cat-Hater lounged between slices of his literary output. A presence, beyond sight and sound, passed into the skin of his being and the molecules of his mind. Like a germ generating an infection, he became immersed in a mass convulsion, induced to knock him down. Knocked down, he had no ground on which to rest his aching feet. Knocked down, his hands reached for a pen and paper on which to complete the poem with which he was to dazzle his impending leadership. Knocked down, he had to keep his eyes upon the phenomenological real. But, his willpower had lost its mind and now obeyed another sign, commanding his hands to inscribe words which Cat-Hater did not understand, "schizo, schizo, get it out." These alien words shouted from the page like a football fan enraged because his team had lost a match. He was no match for this entity, which was fucking around, with his brain chemistry.

Tears soared down Cat-Hater's face. He neither could sit nor did stand, for every movement of his body reminded him that he was no longer alone. I have been taken over. Shaking like a beaten hound, he walked towards the door. He opened it and stumbled outside, trying to externalise the daemon.

The greying streets of Cat-Hater's hometown had once signified fear. Today, they welcomed him. He felt life beneath his feet, air in his hair and saw homes, not houses everywhere he cast his eyes. Each step he took provided a further insight into his consciousness. For although it remained within he was able to justify the daemon's presence.

The devil cannot have me I am bigger than he is; I shall fight until I can live. When he claims me, I shall shame him with a truth to electrify. For I, like a vessel half full of soul, am concealed from the human eye and await filling to the brim. I am just beginning to see within. I travelled beyond the surface and saw that which only truth makers see, its presence in my memory negates the power of he who has taken me. I can feel them pass me forward and backwards like a bottle of gin. Let them drink me slowly. For only I shall win. But, if they bare the same skin, I shall die when they are done. I am distraught with worry, but fear my worries have just begun.

In a flurry, Cat-Hater returned home, ran upstairs and opened the door of his bathroom cabinet. Glaring back were two unopened bottles of tablets, one containing tiny blue pills, the other, tablets coloured white and even more sinister. My sub-cortical defect is a residual affect of having taken such tablets. To avoid the temptation of chemical nullification, he dropped them into a flushing toilet. Plip, plip, plop.

Only when he had no food left in the house, did Cat-Hater venture outside again. He entered his local shop with trepidation, for although everything looked the same he had changed. He grabbed some milk, bread, a tin of tomatoes and even a couple of chocolate bars and exchanged the usual pleasantries with the shop owner, but his hollow smile concealed a nagging feeling that not all was well. He had become an artifice, an outer shell of being, constructed to hide his identity. He was a thought and the thought was a word he was waiting to hear. Although he had avoided eye contact he knew that the shop owner could see the real him.

He turned on the television. The news began with the face of hate, Prime Minister Cameron, the devil incarnate. The newsreader's words blurred into the background like those of a companion in a noisy pub, their content carried away like smoke. Cat-Hater's face became a screwed up mask without a trace of emotion. Vexed from the inside out, he could not even shout for fear of retribution. Supposing the neighbours can hear. Then, Cameron exchanged his face for patterns, which hacked zigzags into Cat-Hater's visual sphere, filling his eyes like sleep he could not wipe away. Everywhere were patterns, he was going blind, but that did not matter; he could always dictate his work.

Four minutes later his vision returned to normal. He ate a little, slept a little and when he awoke wished that he had more weed to smoke. One telephone call and his supplier would have been at his door carrying fuel for his rejuvenation. But, if his phone were tapped, he would be trapped and he was not in the mood for company. He knew that his pursuit of poetry had punished him into believing thoughts he did not believe. Now, was the time to unearth the gold from the debris; it was time to write what he had seen.

Cat-Hater searched for words like a teenage boy trying to chat up girls at a fun fair. Like the girls, words evaded him. He tagged at their skirts and hurt when they ran into the arms of real men. Fighting his own impotence, his left ear opened to the sound of a transmission, which trickled into his eardrum and exploded through the hole, which allowed him to hear. The voice was indistinct, but real. Lasting only seconds, it disappeared like an imaginary friend when adolescence is near.

Cat-Hater withdrew his hand from the area surrounding his ear, where he had felt the swift breeze of words signifying vibrations. Who, whilst I slept, crept into my brain? Is that a microchip I feel in my skull, transmitting the thoughts of those who want to dull my mind like their own? The only crime of which I am guilty is pursuing the secrets of reality. Why have they condemned me so cruelly? The real and the imaginary can only be determined by my sense of duty.

Released from entropy, Cat-Hater picked up his pen. He required being inspired to write an opening line for a novel, which, upon reading, would send fully-grown women and men into waves of adulation in tribute to him. Then he heard a voice, like the scent of a lover's skin, produced to haunt and beguile. "If you could see what I could see, you would be walking this way too." The voice said softly. "If you could see what I could see, you would be walking this way too," Cat-Hater wrote loftily.

Sentences flowed with ease and haste, Cat-Hater wrote the words dictated by him with no face. Like a servant obeying his master, he answered every command; his hand bound around his pen like an instrument of labour, whose produce would ensure his saviour as a giant among writers. He wrote until night became day, free of volition and humbled by the power of dictation. By the time the voice had quietened, Cat-Hater's seed of creativity had blossomed like a youth, profound with truths with which to educate the non-believers.

For three nights, the dictation commenced at eleven o'clock at night and terminated at five o'clock the following morning. Cat-Hater had never felt so happy; his misery more than a distant memory, he knew that he would never feel depressed again. The notation of the sentences of the voice built into a symphony of words, which demanded not only to be heard, but, also, read.

Cat-Hater listened to music and danced the afternoons away, waiting for the hour when his sacred company would come to stay.

On the forth night his sacred company did not call, Cat-Hater fell to his knees like a choirboy. By half past eleven, he felt crushed, looking up to heaven for inspiration to continue his textual communication. Numbed by non-response and abandoned by his former mood of elation, he beseeched the voice to speak. Without your presence, I am too weak to fulfil my destiny. Let me hear your voice and I shall once again be free. Let me hear your voice and I swear that I will worship whatever name you bear. For, even Satan is pure, if you are he.

Cat-Hater looked at his empty armchair, where a vision was pulled from the air, like a stray cloud estranged from its rightful place and repositioned with true care. Reclining like a piece of natural beauty, carved in flesh and blood, sat a figure that would have drawn even the most profane to tears of goodness. Somebody had understood the profundity of Cat-Hater's words, but so lost was he in the wonder of beauty's eyes and lips which threatened to smile, that he almost forgot about his novel. He felt as though he had known the handsome stranger all his life and did not have to ask him his name, for he knew it already, Jude.

Jude began to dictate to Cat-Hater his novel. Cat-Hater grabbed his pen and in awe of his new friend, wrote more than he had ever thought possible. Dialogue was not exchanged; talk is unnecessary when you are the same. But, when the dictation had ended, Cat-Hater looked up and saw that Jude, also, had disappeared. Overcome by fear of aloneness, he prayed for Jude's swift return. I love you so much that my senses burn.

Exhausted, Cat-Hater escaped into sleep. Two hours later, he awoke feeling incomplete and walked into his kitchen to prepare a drink. Perched against the sink was the vision that had pierced his sight, his dark secret, which no one could have guessed, his uninvited guest, whom he would have invited had he known of his existence. Shaking from the inside out, Cat-Hater made two cups of coffee and placed one beside Jude who failed to move, staring ahead as though he could see through the kitchen walls, beyond the world outside Cat-Hater's flat and into a realm remaining inaccessible to all but he, himself. Throughout the day, Jude flitted in and out of Cat-Hater's life, like a moth attracted to his brightness only to be repelled by the dark. He would present in the bathroom, sit on the kitchen table and sometimes even recline on the chair where Cat-Hater had first encountered him. He did not speak and Cat-Hater was too afraid for words, but every time Jude disappeared Cat-Hater's desolation grew more severe. He had made his only true friend and the pain of parting was real.

His novel had been forgotten; he had been torn apart, like cotton, from a cotton reel. I did not hurt before he came, I did not feel. Now, I hurt so much that I am a feeling revealed. He had looked at a stranger and seen himself looking back. Without Jude's presence, he was half the man he had once been, half an identity is an identity lost. "Get up and get dressed." Jude stood over Cat-Hater as grandly as an old oak. Magnificent in his approach, he commanded Cat-Hater. He spoke to me. I shall do as I am told. Cat-Hater left his thoughts behind and gathered up his clothes.

"You are so hungry, your gut is about to burst." Cat-Hater felt his stomach rupture; he was close to fainting, his body a weak and feeble structure. "Get out and buy some food, you idle fucker. The supermarket is practically next door." Cat-Hater found some money and ran to the supermarket so hard that his feet bled red raw. Inside the supermarket, he clenched a shopping basket as though it was his only defence against a fall. He hid his eyes from the prying crowd, which sought his destruction, but each step taken seemed to increase the annoyance in the voice of the one he loved.

Cat-Hater picked up a pizza. "Pizzas are for those who eat shit," barked Jude. Cat-Hater put down the pizza, like a dog mouldy with age. Cat-Hater picked up a bottle of Pepsi. "Pepsi rots the brain," Jude proclaimed. "Buy a cucumber if you want to stay sane." Cat-Hater placed a cucumber in his basket. He hated cucumbers. "Buy five salmon."

"Can I buy lamb instead?" Cat-Hater pleaded.

"You'll become a paedophile, if you don't do what I say." The world is staring at me, because I was always too afraid to go outside and play.

"Come home with me," Cat-Hater sobbed. Jude laughed gleefully. The beauty which, Cat-Hater, formerly believed he had perceived, emanated from deceit, not reality. I have been won over by Satan's smile and am doomed never to be free of his destructive elegance and brilliant repartee.

Everyone is sniggering. I am not a clown manipulating the crowd with smiles of misery. I am not a freak; there is nothing funny about me. He, quickly, traced the sign of the cross in the air, abandoned his shopping and bleeding internally, ran home. The omnipresent image of the malevolent mirage bore deeply into Cat-Hater's bones like a cancer searching for a home. He shouted at him to be left alone, but he only shouted back. He teased Cat-Hater like a school bully aware of his vulnerabilities. "Gay boy." "Bum boy." "You don't know the meaning of fun, boy." Cat-Hater felt that there was no escape; he was doomed to be either the victim of a taunting tongue or a world, which raped his subjectivity. Thus, he chose to hide inside and tackle Jude's accusations headlong.

He transformed every accusation made against him into a taunt against his former friend. Initially there was no reprise, but where there is a beginning, there must come an end. Jude vanished from Cat-Hater's home. Cat-Hater praised God that he was alone, but knew that his life would never be the same and that Jude's absence was purely physical.

Louise M. Hart

CHAPTER THREE

As the week evolved Cat-Hater glimpsed, through his mental haze, the words MOTHER'S DAY above a date on his calendar. Both dismayed and amused he stubbed out his roll-up and waited for the phone call, he could not ignore. The phone call came the following day. He wanted to shut out the ringing tone, to pretend that he was not home, but he knew that she would never go away. If it is not she, I shall listen carefully to the thoughts of the person speaking to me and think violent thoughts, silently. He lifted the phone and said, "Hello."

She was glad that he was well and happy in his job. She was pleased that his cigarette smoking had eased, but she was not entirely convinced that he was eating as well as he should be. Thus, she was pleased that it was his turn to cook for her on Mother's Day. And most importantly, his brother was really looking forward to seeing him.

Cat-Hater wished his Mother goodbye and added a sentence to his work in progress. "He packed his shopping basket with the foods…" And, thus, he went food shopping.

He packed his shopping basket with the foods he had liked before Jude's appearance, but in anticipation of another visitation, his body hummed with fear. He wanted to vanish between the shelves in the shop like a discarded can of sardines. Although free of the cursing tongue, his clothes drained his body of sweat. When he returned home, he collapsed like a mass of skin and bone without density. He prayed a million times that day never again to be betrayed by the artifice of beauty. And never to hear again.

Mothers' Day arrived and he had forgotten her card. The pain in his arm reminded him of his childhood. She entered his home behind his brother who greeted him with a venomous glare, which penetrated Cat-Hater somewhere between his bulging big toes and the tips of his hair. "Aren't you cold?" Enquired Brotherlylove, eyes fixed at Cat-Hater's crotch bound in shorts, perhaps a little too tight to be respectable.

"Cuppa tea, love?" Asked Mother, picking her way to the kitchen past the mountains of overflowing carrier bags and a mound of old newspapers. "Have you got any clean cups?" For dinner, Cat-Hater served pizza and oven chips and for desert, ice cream. "Would you like any cream on your ice cream, Mother?" Her son asked. If you had a womb, I would eat you.

"No thanks, love. I'm on a diet. You're looking well." He had lost a stone in less than two weeks. He tried not to look at her drooping tights and pretended to eat. After dinner, Cat-Hater played his DVD of the film, "Happiness." Mother closed her eyes and pretended to sleep; Brotherlylove played with himself. In his battle to deepen his consciousness, Cat-Hater played out an internal scenario, a scenario more real than the meal he had just eaten, more real than the feel of the words, which were not whispering in his ear, more real than he, himself, had begun to feel.

Cat-Hater: I'd like to slice you in two with a Stanley knife.

Mother: When you grow-up, will you say that to your wife?

Cat-Hater: You took a life and crushed it. I am the product of a squashed tomato; a seed stuck between your teeth. You would like to eat me, but there would be nothing left to press against your tongue. I did myself wrong by singing to your song. You did me wrong by listening.

Mother: You pushed until I only heard actions.

Cat-Hater: Actions are merely fractions of thought, incomplete. You sucked my thoughts out of my head, laid them on your bed and made them yours. Nil of thought my head shank to the point where the point of my existence ended with you. And you, who died before you tried to live, cannot even give enough to be touched by the fucked-up vision we pretend to believe is real. If you half liked yourself, maybe I would learn to forgive.

Mother: I didn't know what to do with you. You came into my life like a bolt from hell and when I threw you to the dogs, they refused to swallow.

Cat-Hater: You never greet me. You rattle at my door. When I answer, you listen to your own answers and ignore me as if I'm out of step with your troupe, the object of ridicule and consternation, who exists to be a fool.

Mother: What was I supposed to do when you wouldn't go to school? You had a good brain. I wanted to be you. You wouldn't give me what I wanted, so I did what I wanted to you.

Cat-Hater: Show me the way out.

Mother: You are a big boy now. Don't shout. I wanted your hand in marriage, but I never even got an engagement ring.

Cat-Hater: Show me the way out. You are devoid of meaning and dead from the inside out. I would like to show you a mirror and watch you hide.

Mother: You were brought up respectably.

Cat-Hater: I hate life. You turned intellectual grandiosity into emotional strife.

In the ever-darkening realm of Mother's Day, his brother's fixed stare and monotonous pacing had increasingly piqued Brotherlylove. "Sit down. It does my head in, when you pace like that."

"That, shat, twat," shouted Cat-Hater; feet moving in synchronicity to the scenario internalised outside.

Mother: You know I love you, love.

Cat-Hater: Like Christ. You stuck me on a cross and forced me above the mass. I am the mass you passed around like slices of bread and butter and laughed at when I stuttered before the whores who bore your family name. My shame is that my blood is the same as yours.

Mother: You were always my little boy; the one I played with until my thrill got too big. Not even a cold shower could erase the impression of your silky skin and your silly, open smile. Let me be your cause.

Cat-Hater: I am a man.

Mother: Let me hold your hand.

Cat-Hater: You have damned my heart.

"You haven't been taking your medication, have you? You're muttering to yourself." Brotherlylove snarled. Due to the eclectic mix and volume of the dialogue surrounding him, Cat-Hater was unable to follow his brother's words, but understood the sentiment.

"Pills will cure your ills. Eat them for breakfast, dinner and supper and you will never suffer. Just do not withdraw, because your balls will turn to rubber," laughed Cat-Hater.

"Mum," shouted Brotherlylove, "go into the kitchen." Mother opened her eyes and whispered.

"Oh dear." She scrambled into the kitchen. "He's not going funny again, is he?" She called out to her sensible son who, with his eyes firmly focused on Cat-Hater, responded not to his Mother, but to his brother.

"Think what it's like for us. I thought you hated hospital. Why don't you take your fucking tablets?" For the first time in over an hour Cat-Hater stood still; he looked into his brother's eyes and drowned in greenness.

"Radioactivity." Cat-Hater yelped, withdrawing into a corner of the room. He had always known that Brotherlylove was Satan's spawn.

"Put your coat on, we're going for a drive," said Brotherlylove. This time Cat-Hater heard his brother's words and dug his nails into the wall like an animal digging for freedom. Blood wept down his hands and dripped onto the floor. He saw the smile in his brother's eyes and knew that his fate had been sealed.

Cat-hater continued to hug the wall like it was the Mother he should have had and daemons visited his world of perceptual green to inform him of his rights. He was Christ, the son of the almighty, whose plight was to save the souls of paedophiles littering the earth with their poisonous seeds. He was the beast, Mr Mephistopheles, a saint among sinners, called upon to spread the creed of the evil deed, masked as goodness. And as goodness, he would succeed in fulfilling the prophecy of the sacred weed, which had unleashed powers he had hitherto not discovered. For the first time his self-hatred had been superseded by love; his was the earth and all who did not live on her. Not living feels good.

In the meantime, Brotherlylove had phoned the local mental health unit and stressing the seriousness of the situation had ensured, after much persuasion, that a posse of individuals with the necessary qualifications paid Cat-Hater a visit. He hurried his Mother into a taxi and remained at Cat-Hater's house, just in case the medics did not perceive the situation as he, himself, did.

Projected before Cat-Hater and dominating every inch of room, Jude's resurrection, resurrected Cat-Hater's own sense of doom. For every look from Cat-Hater was taken up by Jude's deceitful eyes which, reacting to Cat-Hater's continued cries, laughed tears of joy. Then, Jude spoke. Cat-Hater could not understand the joke; the context was indefinable and the punch line did not come until two hours later when a psychiatrist arrived.

By the time Cat-Hater's consultant psychiatrist, a GP and a social worker had arrived, he had run down the road less travelled at least twenty times and found a room of his own. "Hello Jude," smiled Dr Smith-Ghastly. "I'm detaining you under section three of the Mental Health Act." He wondered how the once roly-poly pudding and pie doctor had been able to mutate so easily, a one-time Tom Thumb transforming into Goliath.

He cried, but he did not attempt to run. And Jude's voice rang with rage like an actor on a stage enunciating another person's words. Why, if I am the author, can I not respond with laughter? Cat-Hater could no longer speak; his thoughts subsided into the sound of a squeak audible only to his own sub-conscious.

Imprisoned by distress, Cat-Hater was oblivious to the familiarity of his surroundings, the hospital ward in which he had resided four times before. He struggled with the nurses who held him down on a bed, not to protect himself against the impending injection, but because he rejected human touch. When they touched him, it hurt so much that he felt his psyche had been crushed between their savage hands. Then he felt a sting in his buttock and a sleep of nothingness.

Waking was a slow and laborious process; Cat-Hater's eyes ached with debris, his eyelids weighted to his chest. His head felt as if he had left cognition behind him in a different life, of which he possessed only the faintest memory. He looked down and saw that he was wearing green pyjamas; green pyjamas only mental health units provided. A flow of memory swiftly emerged, which transported Cat-Hater along a field of realisation and culminated in fear. I am back here, between hospital walls. I am well. I should not be allowed on wards.

He wanted to leave his bed and scrounge a cigarette from an unsuspecting virgin of the wards, but feared that the other patients would rage and riot at any attempt he made to engage with their poor, sick presence. He knew that he would not be the only one who did not require pills to relinquish his desire. Deciding to risk the wrath of the hordes pacing the ward, he shakily rose to his feet and made contact with the ground of Quaire Street. YOU CANNOT HURT THE MAN WHO HURTS HIMSELF, BUT...

CHAPTER FOUR

...YOU CAN HURT THE WOMAN WHO DOES NOT.

Nurse Parry worked on a psychiatric ward of the local hospital. She had always lived a full and varied inner life, but not until a moment located between the here and now had she experienced the life of the heart. A look, a gesture, a non-verbal interjection catapulted her out of self and into virgin territory, for in the sexual arena between her eyes Cat-Hater stood out from any other patient ever to be in her care. She worshipped Mother Nature for giving him a face, which fulfilled her yearning for a form of spiritual beauty, which wore its heart on its sleeve and demanded answers to unasked questions. Nurse Parry's first sighting of Cat-Hater provided her with a privileged insight into life itself. "Rape my mind with your tears, Jude," her psyche cried out, "Let me feel truth."

Two days lapsed before the nurse and patient exchanged words. She consumed Cat-Hater's beauty and suppressed the urge to regurgitate the same old dialogue she reserved for less desirable patients. In handovers, her colleagues alluded to Cat-Hater's history of hallucinations. However, to Nurse Parry, the only real hallucination was Cat-

Hater, himself. Her own history of broken relationships, failed marriages, abortions and an ectopic pregnancy informed her belief that, frequently, a smile disguises tears. Finally, after a period of silent communication, the elusive Cat-Hater made his move; he pursued her like a bird of prey, flew into her consciousness and when she turned away she heard him say, "The voices say that they love you." It was not the first time that an utterance of this nature had been said to her, but it was the first time that she had reacted by blushing scarlet from head to toe. Glowing gracelessly, she feigned indifference and tried to avoid his stare.

In handover, she heard herself reiterate Cat-Hater's words to her. "Who is he today," asked Bill, "Jesus or the devil?" Bill rose to his feet, outstretched his arms and, in an effort to disarm his audience with the accuracy of his impersonation, bellowed, "I am the Nazarene." The staff giggled, Nurse Parry congruently laughed along.

She had been unhappily married to Richard for three years. The only fruit of their increasingly seldom-entwined loins was a stain on their sofa, which she had refused to clean in remembrance of things past. She spent her leisure time shagging invisible daemons, whose materialisation led her up alleyways or behind bushes being taken from behind like the mad cow she had become. (Jude, undress my mind and whip me with your eyelashes). Her indiscretions usually occurred on

Friday nights following a few pints with colleagues of invented friendship. One of these was Bill, "You know that Gary from the assessment unit; he's gagging for it. His girlfriend's kicked him out, and, now, he fancies a bit of cock." Nurse Parry embraced the irony of the man whose libidinous focus shifted almost daily and whose conquests, as far as she was aware, were less than negligible. During her student years, she had spent a waking night at Bill's bedside until he recovered from a bad trip. Neither of them had referred to the incident again, brushing it under the carpet with the rest of the neurotic dust strewn along the pathway of their relationship. She was not anti-drugs, in fact, some of her best friends smoked, but she had seen the illness of their effect.

For the next few days, Nurse Parry's life on the wards was comparatively dull, no violent incidents, only the usual non-compliance. She would take a deep breath at the beginning of a shift and exhale only when it was over. Cat-Hater's ongoing experiential ride excluded all others, including, herself, who cursed him for his lack of insight. Stumbling into the nursing office one afternoon, Nurse Soul, the ward manager, recounted an incident during the previous shift when he had been compelled to speak to Cat-Hater about, "his attitude." Seemingly, Cat-Hater had challenged the other patients not only to question the methods of the nursing staff, but also the nature of reality, as he did not see it. To Nurse Soul, the former was awarded primacy. Subsequently, the staff were told to place Cat-Hater on two-minute observations and their fingers on their personal alarms. Nurse Parry had never been the confrontational type, but as she listened to her manager's clinical descriptions of Cat-Hater's behaviour, she decided that she would attempt to discover the motivation behind his apparent distress.

Cat-Hater spent most of her shift pacing up and down, back and forth, coming and going like a horse prior to bolting. Smoking roll-ups with orange peel fingers, he glared at those who dared to look beyond his neck. Nurse Parry approached him with caution, masked as confidence. "Are you in pain?" she asked.

"What do you mean?" His body stalled, eyes pressing into the floor.

"Your expression…you look as of you are in pain." He ignored her as though she were unworthy of a response. Although she hurt, she knew that it was only his illness. (Jude, my bolshy boy, let me tame you until you are strong). Overhearing the nurse, another patient crept up behind her and squealed,

"I've got a pain in my belly." Within minutes Nurse Parry had managed to disentangle herself from the pastry faced neurotic and finally, engage with Cat-Hater on a level, which demanded some form of reciprocity.

"It's not that I am in pain, really. It's the situation I'm in that is making me think…believe…that I am in pain." His voice was forceful, unlike those of other patients who were so heavily medicated.

"What situation is that?" She inquired, "Do you mean that because you're unwell, you think you should be in pain?"

"No, you stupid cow," snarled Cat-Hater. "I meant this fucking hospital." She had said the wrong thing and revealed her true nature, a stupid cow. Her tongue had acted like a thistle, pricking every passing excuse for humanity. Within seconds, cursing the system for turning fine brains into jelly, Cat-Hater overturned the table in the smoke room. The resulting damage comprised delicate streams of fallen ash and dead cigarette butts, which littered the floor like fragmented wounds necessitating attention. Nurse Parry caught Cat-Hater's eye whose expression cut her in two like a blow from a samurai sword. Other nurses had heard the sound of a crash and ran in the direction of the smoking room. Knowing that she was safe from any immediate recriminations from Cat-Hater, she set off her alarm and observed from the sidelines as a crew of her colleagues restrained him.

"I am not unwell," he yelled, as he was led to his bed area, to be given an injection rendering him inactive for the next couple of days. She realised that she had inadvertently handed him his hanging rope, but he had hurt her so. Two days without that face, that body, that mind which she yearned to access. But, she had to show him who was boss. (Jude, why do make Michelangelo's David look like a spotty youth? Why did your beauty yield within me a decisive moment in which I suddenly understood that I was not a healer, but needed healing by you)? Once, she had tried a depixol injection; she could not sit down for a week.

That Friday night differed from most offers, for husband, Richard, had decided to accompany Nurse Parry and her colleagues into the depths and limits of pub land. The nurse secretly questioned his motivation for wanting to join them. Her conveyor belt of thought led her to only one conclusion; he had become suspicious of her infidelity. She hoped that he would not accompany them too often.

Wife and husband shared a bottle of wine. Gulping, she imagined that it was time for reconciliation. But, subsequently, her inner voice informed her that she was letting herself down; she discerned in Richard's expression an aloneness of vision, which pushed her to the periphery of his soul. As he shouted along to a tune on the radio, she contemplated the madness of psychiatry. His vocal chords rebounded against the walls of his throat; she pretended not to notice that they would be late leaving to meet the others. The others worked together, bitched together and drank together. Bill was drunk even before his arrival and sat speeding along with his dead thoughts. A student nurse called Karen, who was mentally barren, looked all dragged up and ready for fornication and John experienced imaginary shags every time Nurse Parry glimpsed the hair on his forearms. Although she was to boast the next day about how he had pressed up against her and ejaculated, her only physical contact with him had been a nibble of a kebab, which he had bought after leaving the pub.

When the Parry's entered the pub, Richard's face dropped like a pair of pubescent testicles and his wife assumed that, like her, he had been struck by the overwhelming vacuity of the situation in which they found themselves. She embraced Bill and pretended to laugh at his idiosyncrasies, Bill just pretended. "How's the job going, Rich?"

"I haven't seen you for ages, Richard."

"Do you miss working at the hospital, Richard? You're looking much better for the job change." Nurse Parry wanted to gag on the hollowness of the souls by which she was surrounded, but chose, rather, to down her lager between sips of white wine and soda. Her eyes strayed beyond the freaks sitting at her table and eventually settled on the lap of a woman sitting in the corner whose legs stretched out to her male companion. As a young woman, Nurse Parry had been a great observer of humankind. Tonight, she wished to recreate her youth.

She noted how the woman at the other table filled

the space between herself and her companion, as she had once done with Richard. She assumed them recent lovers. For the woman radiated the kind of energy associated with the first flush of love and more importantly, the pre-coital desire to please. Nurse Parry imagined herself in a pleasure dome with the woman beside her. Engaged in quiet and considered conversation, the individuals at the other table reclined in one another's minds.

Rachel sipped her vodka and tonic like a virgin on a first date. Seb slapped his larger against his tongue; timing the intervals between gulps of drink, he feared being swallowed by the silences beneath their dialogue. "Take me to your bed," Rachel wanted to say, "Let me lose my lips in the hair on your chest."

"You look horny tonight," stammered Seb's thoughts, "shame you don't fancy me. I wish I was taller."

Nurse Parry became aware that Richard was staring at her; his eyes boring into her skull like a pneumatic drill. She assumed that he believed her to have been eyeing up the rather inconspicuous, bespectacled, short man at the other table. Caught out by the woman's eyes she smiled to herself and shifted her focus to John's forearms.

Nurse Parry drank swiftly and heavily, but not swiftly and heavily, enough to deaden her mind to the list of personal revelations confessed by her friends and to Richard's facial expressions as he ripped the breath out of everyone who dared to express a sexual thought or experience. Her vocalisations became increasingly short and pointed until they vanished altogether. She felt Richard's mildly intoxicated hand on her own and then, she almost liked him, almost, but not quite. "Who's up for some dancing?" He enquired. Everyone stared into oblivion, afraid of living too much.

When the nurse and her husband arrived home, they had sex; it was so good that she almost fell asleep twice; almost, but not quite. The following morning she awoke with phlegm in throat and residual doubts about the previous night. Her job had begun to function like a mental bomb, threatening to explode the possibility of overload; her thoughts, verged on implosion, queuing like patients at the drugs trolley. She decided that she wanted to resign, and then she remembered Cat-Hater.

The next day Cat-Hater stalked down the corridor. "You look a bit stiff," said Nurse Parry, "I'll get you some procyclidine. She hurried to the drugs cupboard and returned with a small, white tablet to ease the side effects of the injection given to him a couple of days ago. Cat-Hater compliantly swallowed the tablet and returned to his room. The next time she saw him his usually immaculately presented curls had been hacked by a blade; nasty bumps and evil tufts littered his perfect scalp, like fungi on the leaf of a perfect rose. (Jude, you are my sick rose). She wanted to lay her hands on his head and resurrect his hair, but remembering the healing power of her hands dared not risk the inevitable outcome of doing so. Cat-Hater's chin glistened with whiskers and his eyes, like those of a raver, hung from their sockets. His obliviousness to his appearance heightened her concern; during the course of two nights, her angel had transformed into a freak. "Would you like some help shaving?" she dared to ask, overlooking the fact that her patient had obviously been in possession of some sort of razor with which he had shaved his head.

Cat-Hater parted his lips and contorted his mouth into a smile beckoning sainthood. He reached into her ear and whispered, "I can do it, myself." Withdrawing, he added a noble, "thank you." He was not suicidal and would not misuse a razor. Thus, the nurse went home that evening and celebrated the invention of anti-psychotic injections.

The following day was her day off work. She cleaned her house and cursed God for not existing. When she had dusted the shelves, she treated herself to a cup of coffee. The aroma tickled her nose hair and advanced into her past life where, her parents, young and in love, soothed her ache of not belonging, by taking her on excursions to parks and zoos. The caged animals resembled her, but she would not have freed them, for their role was to entertain lonely little girls. She smiled aloud, until her smile became a cry; a memory in each tear. Memory became the present and a realisation so unpleasant knocked her to the ground; in the vast congregation of souls, she was numbered beneath one. Had she been beautiful and clever, she might have been numbered above two. Flicking away her tears, she turned on to a television soap opera, bullshitted herself that she was not thinking and decided that, henceforth,

she would only drink decaffeinated coffee.

Crashed down from the skies, Nurse Parry suddenly understood that the sum total of her worth was to support an endless procession of faceless pain; pain that was not psychotic or even sanely neurotic, but dull of effect. She suspected that the patients had seen through her, that they knew that she was no good. If it had not been true, it might have hurt.

"I told the doctor a lie," divulged Cat-Hater. "I'm gay, not bisexual. I've only slept with one woman and that hurt. Do you think I should tell the doctor?"

"You must tell the doctor everything." Nurse Parry tried to gather her thoughts, her heart pumping.

"You think there's something wrong with me. But, I'm so sane it hurts," came his sanity plea. The nurse felt that she understood; her patient needed a woman to show him the one true way. He was confused, mentally ill and not gay.

"Your sexuality is irrelevant to me, but if it's distressing you I'm more than willing to discuss it with you. Do you feel more comfortable with men?" The conversation ended swiftly and the nurse overcame her resistance to reading his medical notes. And, thus, spent the following hour in the splendour of a life reduced to jargon by specialists of the mind whose minds had been reduced.

The reading made hard matter and escalated Nurse Parry's fears for Cat-Hater's plight, for she had not anticipated the extent of abuse experienced by his beautiful being. Her mind swore vengeance. (Jude, you are my prince of tragedy. Make your tragedy mine and in time, I will make you better). Although, it was a proven truth that many psychiatric patients fabricated tales of rape and abuse, her love was greater than the weight of his possible lies. She wanted to rescue someone who did not realise that he needed rescuing and exited the hospital, that afternoon, thankful for possessing a functional mind and eyes that saw more than words on a page.

That evening the nurse could not turn off enough to enjoy a televisual feast; Richard blankly submerged himself in a textbook about cognitive behavioural therapy. She turned her eyes to his mouth, which, like his book, remained open; his teeth stained venous breath tainting the atmosphere with the essence of yellowness. Unaware that her fingernails were stabbing into the thighs of her jeans, she imagined her hands around his neck. Wife and husband squeezed thoughts into the ether which, betrayed by air, adopted silent voices.

Wife: You lump of lard.

Husband: You know you're shit. You have smeared me.

Wife: I hide inside you.

Husband: And so you strayed.

Wife: Oh, behave.

Husband: Like a rampant dog.

Wife: I ride beneath the pregnant pause you secrete when you reach the zenith.

Husband: I'm more like a pussycat without the claws.

Wife: Your wife is a whore, but you get it free.

Husband: Is there no end to the knowing nag that drags you along with it?

Wife: Will there never be an end to you and me?

Husband: Why don't we try again?

Wife: Do you think we would have been friends, if

we had not got together?

Husband: I've tried to understand what those other men see in you.

Wife: What became of the person I was, before I wasn't?

Husband: Like Hannibal, you eat men for dinner.

Wife: I used to be slimmer.

Husband: I used to be slimmer.

Wife: Let's have a hug and pretend that its love that divides us together.

Husband: You sicken me.

Wife: Like glue, your persona sticks to, and binds my liberty.

Husband: I hate me.

Wife: So do I.

Husband: I could kill. They say all men are misogynists; maybe, that's why I married you.

Wife stabbed husband with a Stanley knife. Spurting blood signified the end of a life unworthy of significance. To the delight of the shepherd of death, his shirt glowed no longer white, but crimson. Delicately fingering the cotton, her fingers immersed the redness. She lifted her hands to her nose and inhaled; her tongue flicked against her fingertips and the taste of death inspired her to dance to the beat of a different form of distress, that of freedom of oneness.

"I think I'll go to bed," said Richard. Nurse Parry shook away her phantasy and grunted. Tomorrow promised the gift that was Cat-Hater. She never left a parcel unopened.

"Nurse," called Cat-Hater, "I want to speak to you."

"My name is Brenda," she replied. Sitting on the fag burned chair beside her anti-hero, she awaited his next sentence.

"Do you think my eyes look evil?" Swimming in medication, Cat-Hater's eyes shone like sapphire light bulbs, their electrical undercurrent sparking reactions in the nurse, which even she could not turn off.

"Why do you think they look evil?" She enquired.

"Because it's all in my mind." Lying in bed that night, Nurse Parry questioned why Cat-Hater never used her first name. She was not his nurse, but his secret lover.

"Nurse," called Cat-Hater. "I've written a poem. You can read it, if you like." He handed her a piece of paper and walked away. The poem read as follows:

Invisible beings talking to me

Visions

Complete in disunity

Where will it all end?

Cameras

The all hearing ear

Fuel my fear of involuntary self-disclosure.

Perhaps, I should smash my head

Alternatively, refuse to leave my bed

Maybe medication

Will end my meditations

Perhaps, the secret

Will wither

If I keep it

Until then I shall remain inside out.

I see reality

But reality

Sees

Not

Me

Two hours later the nurse glanced at her patient and promised to discuss the poem with him after she had completed her paper work, for the essence of a nurse's work is written on paper.

CHAPTER FIVE

They call me Jude in here, but my name is Cat-Hater. Mother is the matron of all that I survey. I tried to look into her eyes, but she turned away. Maybe, she sees the evil. My only other visitor has been Che; he bought me a newspaper, which I couldn't read. My mental illiteracy is a consequence of spiritual greed, greed because I used to read too much. He looked at his most butch. I wanted to impress him by trying to undress him, but all I did was tell him that materialism sucks.

Che told me that the American president is coming over here. I said that the president should visit this nut house and stay away from the beer. I wanted to tell him about the real me, but was scared that he already knew what I was about to say. So I tried to hide my thoughts beneath a blanket of external Okays. Due to its weight, the blanket dissolved. I could not concentrate, only hearing beliefs which I had started to hate, like how revolution is brewing in the streets and how I should get better soon in order to participate. I dare not tell him that the revolution has already arrived; mind is my comrade and the cosmos my bride.

I realised today that my life is a post-modern

tragedy. I have no skin, I have no body to hide within, only mind. Corporeal dysmorphia is a belligerent ally. When I was born, I roared like a dying lion. I am no lion, but I am dying; each piece of me grinding down the seconds of time I spend pretending to be alive. There is no cure for me, only suffering. The older I become the more aware I am of the daylight and the dark, the fire and the water, the summer breeze and the winter storm. This awareness fills my waking hours with dreams in which only I believe. But, even worse is the pain of knowing, but being unheard. The ears of fear mute my words. Knowing is a sin in the world of the material, the error which they call reality. Punishment begins from day one.

I was ripped from her womb, torn apart like ripe fruit by the hands of gluttons and directed to the light. The light shone not upon my soma, but through the pores of my thoughts. And the hands bit into my consciousness, which grabbed my jaundiced flesh; like a joint of pork, those around me consumed me. Mother and Father sliced me into pieces and handed me to doctors who never committed me to love and care. I may have lived in my parental home, but I was never all there.

Born into a perceptual misconception, echoing within me was an endless tunnel of thought constructing my inner self; the outer became an imprint of everyone who crossed my path, the inner a consequence of God having a laugh. Who is to blame? All are responsible, for bitter am I.

But, I would rather keep revenge in my head than leave someone dead.

The reason why I am so disliked in the hospital is that I speak truth. Not the Truth, but truth-in-itself. Truth hurts; I am the realisation of the hurting self. My thoughts have been broken bilateralism is a wank. My hospital bed has become my think tank. When happy I am sad, when they think I am sane I am really mad. My words hang falsely in the air, their truthfulness denied by those who pretend to care. Who is testing me? Who takes responsibility for my plight? I denied responsibility, the day they took my rights from me. They placed my rights in a locked drawer with my medical notes and when they observe me writing, laugh as though I am a joke. They will laugh on the other side of their faces when I achieve the revenge of the pen. I doubt that they will even recognise themselves when they read about "they" and "them." One day the world will see that no fucker laughs at me.

Hoping that Che would pop in to declare his undying love, I bathed the other day. A kind woman lent me some bubble bath, which, actually, smelled quite good. I must have used half the bottle, for it bubbled to the rim of the bath. But, she didn't complain when I returned it; she said I smelled more feminine.

He may be married with children, but I am sure that Che is gay. His denial suggests a desire to be led astray. We are spiritually entwined; I look into his eyes and see the reality behind the ideology he tries to espouse. I didn't join the Party because of him; he merely made the journey fun. I pretended to run in order to be caught by a master of the craft of making all opposition seem facile and daft.

I may smell sweet, but that bathroom stenches like shit. A camera placed in the top right hand corner gazed at my genitals to prohibit me from breaking the celibacy order. In World War 2, it was bromide in the tea; here it is chlorpromazine in the water.

At school, they gave the leftovers to pigs; here, we are the pigs. It is nine thirty in the morning, I have eaten two, cold pieces of toast. Three nurses sit with us in the smoking room, but no one speaks. For they are spies of the worst kind, who plant themselves within our intelligence and subsequently express to doctors the content of the thoughts we choose to suppress. I aim for mental nothingness.

Maybe, Che will visit today; I cannot face another bath. My sense of boredom operates like eternity, which cannot last. To drown out the noise I listen to music through my headphones. Every track is a celebration of being me. I glorify the spirits for choosing me to hear the music of my own history. I have tried to tell the other patients about the inverted universe, but they are all too drugged up to realise their own worth.

I had a revelation that my visual perception is a grand hallucination. Beings have no existence beyond my creation; they thrive via my eyes whether in the past, present or future to torture me into believing them real. History is a delusion. I know this, for I am the one who sometimes thinks in rhyme, but, too clearly all the time.

My Mother has arrived. She asks me if I like the food in here. I say that it is very nice, but I miss the beer. She is wearing a green cardigan buttoned to the neck. The temperature, in here, must be a hundred degrees; maybe it has not hit her yet. She says that I am looking better. I smile sweetly and light another cigarette. "Are the nurses nice?" she asks.

"I don't know which one I hate the most," I reply, surprised by my own candour.

"They're here to help you. You must talk to them when you're feeling down." I almost choke, look around and see one standing by the smoking room door. Thirty minutes later my Mother leaves. Surprised I am not relieved; I feel a shudder travel up the base of my spine to the pit of my mind. I shake my head and hear someone say that he wants me dead.

After my Mother's visit, the ward manager summons me to the nursing office. I know that I am about to suffer. I trot behind the manger who wears a pitying smile on the back of his head. "Don't look so sad," I long to say, "I'm not dead, yet." He tells me that he is pleased with my progress, and then hesitates; I become lost in his pregnant pause and contemplate the possible content of his next utterance. Has my Mother a terminal illness? Am I about to taken off my section? No. "Your Mum was worried about upsetting you," he says, "your house was burgled last week. They didn't take much, only some records and an odd C.D."

I bolt out of the office. Music is my lifeline; no music spells death time. The stench of tears infiltrates everywhere I survey; clear rivers of salt appearing as though from another universe dissociated from the outside in. A cleaner looks into my eyes and her kind mouth offers sympathy to this fruit whose lack of nuts has been revealed in a cry. "Do you want me to get a nurse?" she asks.

"It's okay," I splash, "they'll think I'm putting it on." I throw myself on my bed and think of Jesus Christ, cherry pie, the stars in the sky and every smile Che has directed my way. By the time, my name is called for my next dose of medication I have dusted down my blotched cheeks. Gulping down my tablets, I realise that mad people cry; when I shed those tears I waved my sanity goodbye. In the evening, I write a poem. I think I shall show it to the weirdo nurse. She is as dead as a Christmas duck and the education would be beneficial to her.

CHAPTER SIX

There is a spectre haunting the western world and that spectre is a concept, the concept of sanity. From the Royal palace to the council houses of Foleshill, Coventry brain cells are imploding through the desire to belong. The arms of (hu) man are bound by a system of control, a system of control boundlessly not human. A shadow hangs above our nations; externally it is orange and purple, within it is black and grey. Intangible in texture, it swallows completely all those who dare to challenge its nature. Like a challenger divorced from his celestial home, Cat-Hater's descent was doomed to be grounded on earth, for all challengers are sentenced to live without answers.

It was ward round day, time for Dr Smith-Ghastly to round up those sheep, which had gone astray. Cat-Hater tried to smooth his brow. Knowing that the omniscient eye was forever upon him, he forced down his throat an extra piece of toast and looked up to heaven for guidance as to how to approach the fat lapped doctor. He observed the doctor's first victim, escorted by the weird nurse; walk towards the room of doom where he knew the guardian of loon would question the other patient. The radio played one of the latest dance tunes. A fellow traveller danced like an elephant at a rave.

Cat-Hater had concluded that Coventry in

England, his ostensible home should be removed from the map of the world. The abode of all he despised, he desired to be free of her people and her watchful C.C.T.V. eyes. He had been formed to reside in the realm of the east, where spirituality suffices from princes to beasts; he would follow the desires of his mind and construct a plan to extricate himself from the nightmare of the nuthouse.

Coventry City located in the middle England of nowhere houses a psychiatric hospital and a Cathedral. Beside a daycentre for adults with mental health issues lie premises of the Jesus Army, where delusions are transformed into miracles for the price of a free cup of tea. Staff at the psychiatric hospital are reluctant to make their patients coffee. Thus, Cat-Hater had taken to drinking tea twice a day with his nostrils closed.

Being on the inside, Cat-Hater was barely aware that people had begun to question. The answers are nearer today than yesterday. Each day is a blessing when the world has cancer. As the tumour grows, truth unfolds; death is a life enhancer. And the Revolutionary Socialist Party, seeing blood on the hands of this merciless State, has continued their plans to render the world a more egalitarian place. Positioned in their secret dens, Party members plot their moves and then...

Che looks very fetching in grey. Today, he held a caucus to discuss the burgeoning unrest of those opposed to austerity measures and Tories whose demeanour suggests a smell under their noses. Communicating with his comrades has revitalised his plight to succeed as a future leader of a society whose apparent greed is a product of a system based on capital, not need.

Since his detention in hospital, Cat-Hater has not watched television. He has not seen the footage of people on the streets or heard the voices of dissent, except those satanically sent to him. In contrast, Nurse Parry became a tele addict the second she reached her honeymoon suite. Last night, a pillaging crew flashed upon television screens; Coventry became a Marxist's wet dream. Even television bias lent notable allowance to the views of the left. In hospital, Cat-Hater blinks his eyes. For him there is no tomorrow for which to fight, only endless days.

Nurse Parry approached Cat-Hater a little tentatively, for she still had not read his poem. She had been given, after all, a ream of paper work to complete and poetry had never been her forte; she could not recall having read a poem since she had left school. "Jude," she smiled lovingly, "the doctor wants to see you." Cat-Hater's bowel rumbled aloud, he tried to stand tall, but his shoulders let him down. He walked behind the nurse and tried not to frown. Upon reaching the door of the office Nurse Parry turned to him and said, "when the ward round's over, we'll have a chat about your poem."

"I hope he isn't nasty to me," Cat-Hater emoted. "If

he is," he thought, "I'll pull his head off his shoulders."

"Such vulnerability," thought she, "nearly brings me to my knees."

Sitting in a broken semi-circle of faceless faces, Cat-Hater was forced to confront his nemesis, the doctor, whose smile inflated his face like a pump filled with hot air. Nurse Parry sat in cross-legged anticipation; Cat-Hater's notes perched on her knees. A junior doctor lapped up the scene, whose name he did not remember. He recognised the other face as that of an occupational therapist. She had never been present at his previous review meetings. Was this a sign that he was to be re-introduced to pottery sessions and art materials? Was his mental health to be measured in terms of his dexterity and, more frighteningly, the products he would create in these sessions?

"How are you?" The doctor's eyes sprinted towards Cat-Hater's hands, which, immediately, adopted a tremor.

"I'm very well doctor."

"How are the voices?" Doctor Smith stroked his blue tie, like a penis extension. Encased in his blue suit was a shirt, which shone like white lightening, his jacket failing to conceal his mountainous paunch.

"I don't hear voices. I've told you before."

The voice of the people produces an echo; it begins in thought and ends in action. A contagious ally demanding beings to obey commands, the voice has discovered a universal ear commanding all possessors to do as they hear. The strength of the voice lies not within the words it speaks, but in the force with which it is heard. The force, among those so inclined, was to depose The State and introduce a right old state.

"What do you think about?" Smith-Ghastly, enquired.

"The corridors between the City walls echo with the sound of torment. Young and old speak in tongues and eat without forks; they talk of pain preceding pleasure. Never a dull word is left unspoken, never a tear unshed. They wish themselves dead only because they know that the afterlife is here. And in the student halls beer cans rub up against saucers. For interaction is protection against aloneness. In the city centre, Peeping Tom's venture to give all a thrill ends in late night brawls. They hide behind their bloody masks the transience of their lives and the pathways they follow to annihilation. But we who have history cut our throats every second day, for we wonder why the oppressed try to find a way out. It is what life is all about...The corridors between the city walls echo with the...

"Brenda said that you liked poetry," smiled the doctor. Cat-Hater's frown dissolved into a smile whose irony eluded everyone. He glanced at the nurse who, although insecure that her smile would not equal the radiance of that of Cat-Haters, smiled back like a Cheshire cat from Coventry. "You seem a little high," continued the doctor.

"High!" Cat-Hater could not disguise his sense of disbelief. "I'm depressed. I was born into this world screaming and have never stopped."

His funeral would be a grand affair, attended by all those who did not care. Mother and Brotherlylove walking with heads lowered behind the coffin. His only ever girlfriend would grab a front pew and pretend that she was not looking sideways at his family, yearning to be recognised. His shell greeted by the familiar chords of, "Who wants to Live forever," by Queen would prompt a universal tear from the downcast congregation who had been cast down. Rising to untidy emotion, some would remember, others regret their part in his death. Not among these would be the hospital representative whose only sadness would concern the terminal nature of Cat-Hater's illness, which, she knew, she would never catch. Sitting at the back, three learning-disabled service users, would struggle to sing the hymns and notice that they were the only people dressed in black.

"I think we'll increase your medication. Just a little," asserted the doctor.

"I am a walking indictment of a mental health system which turns saints into monsters," cried Cat-Hater from somewhere deep inside, words buried so far within that they failed to surface outside.

"Sarah will talk to you later about starting an O.T. programme and I'll see you next week."

Sarah, a typically young and pretty occupational therapist approached Cat-Hater with typically young and pretty enthusiasm and handed him a sheet of questions on which he was asked to record his personal experiences and highlight the activities in which he would like to participate. Cat-Hater did not intend to inform his captives about his personal experiences. Occupational therapy, however, took place outside the ward and would allow him to escape from the lime green walls, which had surrounded him for the last month. After agreeing to participate once a week in an open, art session and a creative writing session, Cat-Hater's anger with the doctor began to dissipate. He picked up a pen and wrote his own notes.

So what is to become of Jesus, born in Stoke Aldermore, Coventry, christened in allusions, a delusion to those who cannot see? He stops banging his head against rubber walls. He begins to realise that the evil in his eyes has been caused by medication. He decides that practising meditation may yield an even more fluent reality. He knows that the cure is not a chalky tablet, but a tablet of stone written by his own hand. He knows that his journey has been planned. He wonders if he is I.

Louise M. Hart

CHAPTER SEVEN

She says: I liked your poem. All writing that's real is good.

He says: What if it wasn't real.

She thinks: I had better think of a clever response quickly.

She says: Then it wouldn't be authentic.

He thinks: She's more stupid than I thought. I could have copied a Shakespearean sonnet and she wouldn't have guessed that I had not written it.

She says: There seems to be a lot of negativity in the poem. Would you like to work on that?

He says: I've been working on that my whole life.

She says: It must be exhausting.

She thinks: He's starting to open up. I might achieve something here.

He thinks: This woman is seriously fucked up.

She thinks: Look at his gorgeous eyes. I could eat him for supper. I have to get round to discussing loneliness.

She says: I think you're lonely.

He thinks: Why do nurses believe that they have the right to make over-generalisations about their patients. I'll get her back.

He says: Aren't we all lonely? What did you think of my poem?

She says: I liked it.

He says: I know that you liked it, but what did you think of it?

She says: I thought it was thought provoking.

He says: You mean it was shit.

She thinks: Help. He's getting angry. Better, be careful what I say. I'll tell him how I enjoyed his use of words. I just wish I could remember some.

He says: You think I'm mad.

She says: No, I don't believe that anybody is mad.

He says: I do. Mental illness is the medicalisation of madness. Why not get back to basics. Remember that even when you are standing on the other side of the room I can hear what you are thinking.

She thinks: He always denies to doctors that he hears voices, but he has just admitted it to me again.

She says: What kinds of things do you hear me say?

He thinks: She's trying to catch me out; make out that I'm hearing voices to cover her own back.

He says: Are you deaf? Can you not hear what you think?

She says: Maybe I've got a short memory.

She thinks: I'm getting clever.

She says: So what am I thinking now?

He says: Fuck all.

She thinks: At least he doesn't think I'm thinking horrible things about him.

She says: In the ward round you said that you were depressed.

He thinks: The doctor has told her to find out if I am suicidal.

He says: Your husband used to work up here. I remember him from years ago.

She says: Richard! How do you know...?

He says: People talk.

He thinks: I don't plan to do away with myself. I was talking about the circle, repetition, medication, incarceration. On and on, in and out of hospital.

She thinks: If he stayed on medication, he might be able to live a reasonable life.

He says: Yes, I did stop taking my medication. Now look at me, I am taking it again and I am totally depressed. Is this your reasonable life?

"I've just been talking to that nurse wearing the blue jumper," Cat-Hater sulked to a patient wrapped in a Mac of worries, his eyes wearing the expression of a cat locked outside on a rainy winter's night. He skulked into a seat in the smoking room. "Mental rape," he hissed, heading towards the bathroom to purge himself. Nurse Parry spent the rest of her shift smiling.

CHAPTER EIGHT

Nurse Parry had to buy the flowers herself, for she had no servant to steal them for her. Musing among the petals, she was attacked from the back by a wave of thought about Cat-Hater, who made life not so bad. (Jude, you could prove to be my undoing). "I prefer flowers to men," she whispered beneath her breath. "Except Jude."

Waves slapping the shore of her consciousness, she listened until her breath grew heavy. She was not lonely, just desperate. Unaccustomed to holding dinner parties, she had left the preparations until the last moment; the day it was to be held. Although she had resided in Coventry most of her life, she still delighted in the spectacle of watching the figure of Peeping Tom pop out beneath the face of the Lady Godiva clock at the stroke of the hour. Smiling, she stroked a carnation. As she walked through the city centre, she recognised the face of a former patient and fixed her gaze on the space above his head, hoping that he would not attempt to talk to her. Ignoring a friendly, "hi," she strode on in apparent oblivion.

Later in her trip, in a hurried state, she almost knocked to the ground one of the guests invited to that night's party. Piqued to be confronted with the reality of the impending party, the nurse secretly wished that she had been able to inadvertently break a bone or two in the now feather light body of Julie Apple, one time psychiatric nurse, and currently, cognitive behavioural therapist and unfit Mother. "Julie, you look really well," she said, sincerity fleeing from every pore of her caged being. "Are you still coming tonight?"

"Definitely. I've been looking forward to it. How are you, anyway? Bill was telling me about Richard's new job. Oh, those flowers are lovely." The two women spent two minutes disengaged in meaningless chat. When they had parted, Nurse Parry questioned why she had invited to her house someone of such intellectual barrenness. Nurse Parry was a winner, why should she associate with someone who made her look fat.

The waves refused to stop. Overcoming the eye of her mind, she blinked until her tear ducts streamed lashes of flashes of thought, which she refused to summon to the precipice. Rather she chewed it up, spat it out and pretended to be happy outside with all the plebes from whom she sought to hide. Bravely, she ventured into a café where she bought a cup of cappuccino and a cream scone. Contentedly anonymous among the other faceless customers, she allowed her mind to lapse into the phantastical. The pseudo woodland behind the hospital building morphed into a forest; wild in the wilderness of the eyes of those it summoned, it called her beyond the ward and seduced her at the feet of its billowing trees. The ground onto which she fell, felt raw with leaves and twigs. She dragged Cat-Hater down with her, her hands reaching for flesh beneath his clothes, she married her juice to his, in a ceremony lasting minutes, not seconds and they rose together in temporal truth.

(Jude, you are my bride. Lucifer of tongue, with Christ inside. You do me in and open me up. Approaching me from behind, you resurrect your locks and drown my mouth in sin and cock. I eat your flesh and am so impressed that I shake. I cover you in breast. You say that it is your favourite part of a bird, so I twitter and coo. You have fulfilled my dream to fuck the Nazarene. A virgin in the clothes of a whore, I undressed you, saw your truth and it was not holy).

Like a sudden crash of a wave upon a shore, the realisation dawned that she had just had sex with a patient, it may have been mental sex, but was that, really, more acceptable than the physical act? She knew that thoughts often functioned like playful imps, leading beings to trespass into temptation; however, like imps they were, also, illusory and therefore powerless when dismissed. She smiled and imagined Cat-Hater sitting opposite her. He would gulp down his can of coke while she delicately nibbled her scone and sipped her steaming cappuccino. He might be brave enough to share her scone, for he was not a big eater. "I love you," he would whisper, wiping a smudge of cream off his lips.

She felt him press his knees against hers and lifted her foot to the bulge in his trousers. Roused from her imaginings, she noticed that two women sitting at another table were staring her way. When she caught their eyes, they looked at one another and began to giggle. The sound of their giggling seemed to reverberate around the café. Leaving the remains of her drink, the nurse nervously left the café.

Nurse Parry suddenly remembered that she had to cook a meal and dashed into a supermarket. She had never been a proficient cook, opting, rather, to live off microwave meals. She could cook, however, a good curry with tinned sauce. Thus, she bought a tin of madras sauce, some chicken breasts and made her way home. Driving home, she stopped at traffic lights, where a woman crossing the road caught her gaze. Despite her denim attire and facial piercing, the woman displayed whippet like grace in advancing towards the pavement. The nurse wished that she had the courage to wear her hair so short. Focusing on the shapes the woman made with her frame in the simple act of walking, she was blind to the inelegant turn of her own lips, her moronic smile greeted by the violent action of the woman's middle finger raised in the air. Nurse Parry drove on and fighting against tears, thought of Jude.

Crossing the road behind the woman, Seb and Rachel headed for the other side. He saw a portent in the red traffic light of danger unrelated to the oncoming traffic; she took the upper hand and hastened him across the road, for he had become so slow recently. When his feet hit the pavement, she sighed with relief and escorted him to a park, where he could sample the delights of nature, inaccessible to him in the confines of his stark bed-sit. A psychiatrist had prescribed Seb anti-depressant medication, but Rachel had seen no improvement in his health. She sensitively suggested that he might like some support at his next doctor's appointment. He said that he felt tired and sat on a bench.

Sitting beside him, Rachel tried to distract Seb from gazing at the grey clouds, which enveloped them like a huge blanket, but every word she spoke disappeared into the breeze and he continued to focus on something, which she was glad she could not see. "The clouds are as one," his mind repeated, "an individual no one sees. I have tried to be good. I am never me."

"Seb," called Rachel, "Seb. Do you think I should make another appointment for you? I think four weeks is too long for you to wait to see a doctor."

He had recently returned home from the war on terrorism. He had joined the army at the age of seventeen, when at the end of the Thatcherite 1980's, the only career for a healthy; working class lad with few academic qualifications was in the armed forces. Rachel disliked soldiers and opposed war. Consequently, he had omitted to tell her that he had been in a soldier and, had even fought in the, "immoral and illegal war," towards which she exhibited such contempt. Neither did she know that he had witnessed the killing of his best friend, Bob Titmus, womaniser extraordinaire and bastard son of Sylvester Stallone's Rambo.

Rachel grabbed Seb's hand and placed it on her lap, where the other hand joined it, and was gently rubbed back to life. He wondered if she would be sitting with him, had she known that he were a legal murderer. They both rose to their feet and Rachel walked Seb home.

When Nurse Parry arrived home, her husband greeted her. "Where the fuck have you been? They'll be here at half seven, it's nearly five now."

"I've been buying the food. It won't take long to make a curry," his wife replied, feigning enthusiasm. She knew that Richard could not understand why she had decided to hold a dinner party, neither did she. He sat reading a newspaper; she stood above a stove, the smell of her own cooking threatening to expel the lining of her stomach. Leaving the curry to simmer in a pan, the nurse searched in her wardrobe for a suitable outfit to wear. She grabbed a pair of black trousers, a colourful blouse and began to undress. Dressed only in her underwear, she surveyed her reflection in her bedroom mirror; flooded with anxiety, her heart skipped a beat, for the fleshy mass standing before her not only undermined her sense of self, but challenged the accuracy of her perceptions. Like a clown without his make-up, her identity had been denied. She pinched her substantial thighs and held in her stomach so tightly that exhalation inflicted emotional pain. Gathering herself into her trousers, she managed to overlook her bulging stomach, but having struggled to wrap around her blouse, was forced to acknowledge the existence of surplus flesh. Nurse Parry changed her outfit. "Do I look okay?" she asked her husband.

"Fine," he replied, his head still buried in a newspaper. Richard did not change his outfit.

At 7.31 p.m., Julie Apple rang the doorbell. An expensive bottle of red wine in her hand, obviously, she had not been out recently. "How are you Richard? Do you need a hand with anything, Brenda? The flowers are lovely."

Arriving twenty minutes later, Jo and Joe, glowing like worms in a show of togetherness, handed Richard an expensive bottle of red wine. Julie Apple tried to hide behind her flushing cheeks, but was observed by the nurse, who framed the moment, in her eyes, like a camera lens. Everyone knew that the two Jo(e)s had been out recently, for they both spent the evening describing every detail of their recent social intercourse.

Time dragged on into minutes; at 8.15, her final guest still had not arrived. Nurse Parry wished that it was tomorrow and that she had not lied about cooking the curry from an authentic Indian recipe. Finally, the doorbell rang. The nurse rushed to the door, where she was greeted by Bill's drunken drawl. His hands clenched carrier bags brimming with cans of lager. He staggered into a silent space of guests who were, perhaps, a little too eager for spectacle. "It's like a morgue in here," he quipped, "and you thought she was going to bring out the dead, until I arrived." Julie Apple fell off her perch and laughed so hard that Nurse Parry thought she would be required to activate her CPR skills.

"Bill, it's good to see you're feeling better," said the Apple. Nurse Parry wondered what had been wrong with Bill, but refused to indulge him by asking. Richard lifted his head above carpet level and looked at his wife, who remained expressionless. Usually monosyllabic, in the last few days, Richard's conversations had degenerated into mere grunts acknowledging her existence.

The curry was served and eaten around a dining table, which had been used only four times in two years. They all claimed to have enjoyed their meal, but, despite her modest assertion that it was not, "one of my best," the nurse knew that even Bill, in his intoxicated state, could have prepared a better meal. Scrutinising the Parry's music collection, Bill pulled out a middle-aged CD of the songs of the 1980's, which Richard had bought in one of his rare moments of recklessness.

"I can guess who bought this," barked Bill. Watching him insert the CD in the stereo, the nurse became aware of a feeling of unease, which she could neither explain, nor felt able to articulate to the friends in her house, for Bill was too camp to be himself, Richard had drunk himself into a slumber and Julie Apple had, seemingly, become Bill's best friend overnight; their exchanges indicating knowledge of mutually exclusive information, prohibited from all others. Only the two Jo(e)s remained themselves.

External to the drunken interaction, Nurse Parry clinked her glass of tonic water against the air and watched her friends partake of revelry in which only their psyches were at stake. Their drunkenness predisposed them to believe that her glass contained vodka; she did not suggest otherwise, for she did not want to indulge in the idiocy of the scene. Smug with objectivity, she made all the right noises in all the right places and enjoyed the lucidity of her own thoughts. She wondered if Cat-Hater drank alcohol, then decided that Gods did not drink, did they?

Why had she been thinking in black and white? She could not be depressed; she was a psychiatric nurse. Her body jolted when the rat came out to play. "Let's play truth or dare," they all heard Julie Apple say. Her squeaks demanded to be drowned in a hand of sawdust and poison, but Nurse Parry only had small fingers. Richard crossed his arms and, like a schoolboy, grumped.

"I'm not playing." The others were enthusiastic. Nurse Parry smiled, satisfied that any thought, any experience, which she was about to disclose, unlike those of her guests, would emanate from sobriety. Julie Apple spun a bottle. When it ceased to spin, it pointed in Jo's direction.

"If you could shag anyone in the world, any film star, pop star, celebrity, anyone, who would it be?"

"Johnny Depp."

"Brad Pitt."

"That weather girl from ITV."

"Me," laughed Bill.

Nurse Parry thought hard and decided to choose the second man on her list. "The guy who played Jesus, in Jesus of Nazareth. Remember that from the telly?"

"How old were you when you lost your virginity?"

"I was fourteen. I did it with Sharon Spencer in my bedroom. I told her that if she wanked me first, she wouldn't get pregnant. She didn't, thank god," answered Joe.

Nurse Parry wanted to scream out that, she could have been Sharon Spencer, that all women were Sharon Spencer, that Sharon Spencer was the original model for male abuse. She abhorred Sharon Spencer for representing truth. As though afloat in a lake of fire, invisible flames surrounded her interior. She was a queen in a society of serfs; serfs to their own images, her companions spoke only to the otherness, which affirmed them. An almighty wave threatened to knock her off her pedestal, for she could not distract herself from the image of her husband, paralytic with alcohol, small and twisted in a display of pain.

"I was seventeen, when I lost my virginity," she recounted, "it was one of the most painful and liberating experiences of my life." The game continued, until even Bill became bored. Eventually, Jo and Joe departed, leaving behind the others to laugh and talk about them. The nurse noticed that Richard had failed to engage with Bill all night, continuing to drink heavily. Although, Bill frequently irritated her, he was a necessary irritant and the source, for herself and her husband, of much entertainment. Hoping that her remaining guests would get the hint and go home, she collected their plates and advanced to the kitchen to wash them. Julie Apple followed her, which prompted Nurse Parry to accentuate the extent of her tiredness. She, subsequently, rebuffed her friend's offers to wash the dishes. "Shall I order a taxi?" Said J.A. hearing the irritation in the other's voice.

"Yes," she snapped, in response. Whereupon, Julie Apple pulled out her mobile phone and ordered a taxi.

"It must be good to have a partner you trust,"

remarked Julie Apple, before tumbling into a taxi with her new best friend, Bill. Richard, who had drunk himself sober, sat staring at the mark in the wallpaper, where he had once thrown a mug in anger at his wife for having flirted, unashamedly, with a teenage neighbour.

"Fancy a coffee?" She asked her husband, who answered affirmatively. The morbid cast of her husband's face struck the nurse. "You've been very quiet tonight," she said, pleading for an explanation. He shrouded himself in eerie silence and, suddenly, she realised that there, really, was something wrong; her imagination had not been malfunctioning. She paused for thought. "You haven't fallen out with Bill, have you?

"No," he replied, a little too quickly. "There's something I've been meaning to discuss with you." Briefly, she thought she saw a tear form in his eye. "It's not working, is it? I mean, everyone knows that there have been other men; not just one or two either."

"Have you met someone else? Asked Nurse Parry, incredulous at what she was hearing.

"Not really…it's just confirmed what I already knew about myself."

"Do I know her?"

"No. Well, yes…in a way. But, that's irrelevant.

"Who is it?"

"Bill." Her initial sense of surprise evolved into one of shock. "It was a one off. You know Bill; it will be all round the hospital soon. We aren't in a relationship...Bill, and me but I've wanted it for so long. Not necessarily with Bill, but...with a man."

"You are telling me that I'm married to a puff and I didn't even know." The nurse thought of Julie Apple accessing, assimilating and, subsequently, regurgitating every detail of her husband's sexual exploits with Bill, and felt sick. Soon, everyone would know; she felt even sicker. She was to become a living obscenity, the woman who could not satisfy her man, the laughing stock of ward D3. "Was he better than me?" She asked.

"Yes." Richard went upstairs to bed and glancing behind him, shouted, "as soon as you've found somewhere else to live, I want you out." She made another coffee and decided to move out the following day.

Her only companion, that night was a lamplight, which cast yellow shadows against white. Her thoughts broke into the shadows and enlightened her mind with images of death and life. Death was like her existence, threatening decay in the wake of a husband, friends and an occupation, which sought her moral negation. Life was a being, in a hospital bed, coiled on a plastic cover. Unlike this being, she could make choices. Thus, she selected a carnation and, gently, pulled out its petals one by one. "He loves me. He loves me not." When the last remaining petal correlated with a, "he loves me not," she tore off the head of the flower and whispered, "He loves me." She could make choices and life was hers.

Rachel telephoned Seb to remind him to go to bed, for he had little concept of time nowadays. Then, unable to sleep, she sat before her television clasping a mug of hot chocolate. She hoped that he was sleeping sweetly. Seb, dressed in a coat and doctor martin boots, read a passage from, "Catcher in the Rye." He puzzled about why Salinger had written biographical details about his, Seb's, life in a novel, which pre-dated his existence. John Lennon's, "Imagine," played on the radio.

CHAPTER NINE

Leaning against the wall of the smoking room, Dave Thomas appeared hungry for mischief. Although his aquiline features appealed to Cat-Hater's aesthetic sensibilities, he knew that this was one hetero to whom he should not mention his sexuality. He had first met Dave during his first hospital admission seven years ago and was pleased to see that, unlike many of the other patients he had met over the years; his unkind life had not marked his physical beauty. "A white bloke gets his cock out to piss in the toilets. It's got a tattoo on it that says, "Welcome to England." A black guy, next to him, gets his cock out as well, it says, on it, "Welcome to Jamaica, have a nice day." Cat-Hater let out a belly laugh, his first for some time. Dave's jokes were only acceptable in mixed company, that is, company that was mixed up in-itself. For beyond the walls of the hospital, Cat-Hater would have scoffed at the offensiveness of Dave's humour. In the hospital, the tiniest glimpse of humour stood out like a star in the midnight sky and reminded all that, where there is darkness, there is, also, night.

When you exist in solitude inhabited by people trying to be sane, a ward is a lonely place. Pain is more enduring, more acutely felt. Cat-Hater had been living within himself. Thus, Dave had touched a place, a neglected space, which Cat-Hater had, formerly closed, its re-opening, re-opened himself. He could, after all, react to and interact with, his surroundings. He realised that he had been lost in an illusion that his social being had died. A touch had revived his spirit and opened his mind to the possibility of belonging again. He was a writer in search of a friend.

Every step Cat-Hater took was recorded in text. The story of his life would survive beyond his death. For, like Madame Bovary, he lived to self-textualise. His life had been realised through his power of pre-cognition. Whilst he possessed forethought, he had no control over his life conditions. His existence, merely, was the precondition for a greater story.

The never-ending boredom of it all. Days running into one, like pathways with no terminus. Medication dispensed at prescribed times. Meals served, like fodder, to queuing cattle. Slurps and gulps, followed by burps of regurgitation and boastful farts. Uniformity, uniformly served to those who, like naughty children or lawbreakers, had trespassed beyond demarcation. Cigarettes smoked to pass away the seconds. Conversations blunted by non-response. Responses blunted by pharmacy. How does one hasten the ticking clock? What do you do to improve your lot, when your lot has been seized from your possession and attributed to your imagination?

Cat-Hater's imagination had been stirred by

Dave's activities. By the second day of his admission, Dave had become a dog. When his barks were ignored by the staff, he tried howling, thinly masking his laughter. The staff continued to ignore him. When a nurse called Cat-Hater for teatime medication, Dave crouched on his hands and knees and wagged his invisible tail. Delirious with excitement, Cat-Hater looked at the nurse standing by the medication trolley. "Ignore it. He's putting it on." Said the nurse, annoyance engraved on every line of his face. It was not difficult to piss them off.

The following day, Dave tried to hang himself. Standing in the smoking room, Cat-Hater heard an almighty crash. Within seconds, another patient had entered the room and described how Dave had tied his clothing to the curtain rail around his bed and inserted his head through a loop. Cat-Hater suppressed his reflex to laughter and tried to register shock. For the next twenty-four hours, Dave endured one to one observation by a nurse who followed his every move, including those made in the toilet. Never intimidated, he used every opportunity to piss them off further. Whenever the public phone rang, reserved for the use of patients, he would spring to his feet and answer the call saying, "Hello, nut house."

Cat-Hater decided to quiz Dave about the year he had previously spent a in a medium secure unit. "It must have been terrible."

"It was alright," said Dave. "They did more for you

there, than they do here."

"Did you have therapy?"

"Yeah."

"Why did you go there?"

"I stabbed some nonces." Lost for words, Cat-Hater did not know whether to pity or despise his friend. Eventually, he concluded that he had been hallucinating. A few hours after the nurse had been removed from Dave's taunting; he tried to hang himself again. The sight of a hysterical nurse, charging along the corridor, beckoning her colleagues for help, brought most of the patients out of their shells. Apparently, this time, Dave had tried to end his life in the shower. Once again, he was put under observation. One week later Dave was discharged from hospital. The following evening he telephoned Cat-Hater and suggested that he might like to meet him for a drink, when he, too, had been discharged. Cat-Hater knew that they never would.

After Dave had been discharged, all colour left the ward. A young woman was admitted; whose suicidal ideation was a direct consequence of a relationship break-up. When, only a few days later, she was discharged, the grey cloud hanging above her, burst into a thousand tears of disappointment. She returned within a week with kidney damage, caused by an overdose of tablets, and bearing a scar on her throat. These pseudo-suicidal people filled Cat-Hater's mind like pointed nails and jagged pebbles.

If they were to leave, I could breathe again. Their presence poisons the atmosphere, like need. Their pretend beckoning to the reaper cheapens them and terminates their emotional lives. Those whose minds are filled with air do not bow to the force of subjective despair they merely do not care. I, too, have air, but I wear it around me, not within. I wish that woman would realise that confinement is more stressful than living a lie. She has not been sectioned; she could walk out anytime. Why does she not leave the mentally ill behind? She is the only one, in here, who is truly insane; people, like her, give people, like me, a bad name. Like her, I will never change my perceptions.

Sitting with Cat-Hater, in the smoking room, Elaine, who had lent Cat-Hater the bubble bath, had just recovered from a regular bout of hysteria. She tried to feed him a pot of yoghurt, which, she, already, had half eaten. Women in a psychiatric hospital were problematic; because men had abused so many of them, they were, often, either vengeful or shit scared of their male counter-parts.

Bryan: Gloria was raped, I really fancy her, but she will not have sex.

Claire: I was raped when I was seven.

Bryan: She was raped, something like…ten times.

Claire: I've been raped more times than that.

Bryan: It hasn't stopped you shagging.

Claire and Bryan threw themselves at one another, like feral cats scrapping over a morsel of food, which, though decaying, represented the only possibility of nourishment on a bare pantry day. Pulling them apart, like retracting elastic, the nurses smiled smugly when, eventually, their patients retreated to their respective corners. Cat-Hater wanted to shout, "It's happened to me as well," but he was a man.

Elaine asked Cat-Hater if, like her, he had a single room, rather than a bed in the dormitory. He said that he had.

"Have you noticed the distorting mirror?" He asked, "I think there is a camera behind it."

"It's made of plastic," said Elaine.

"You mean, so that we can't cut ourselves. You have to be careful, in here, you know; the staff room is right behind this room. I bet they sit in there listening to us. They are probably listening now. Bitches."

"Bitches," repeated Elaine. "They're always coming into this room to snoop, as well."

"I hate the fat one, the weirdo with the long hair and glasses. She follows me around," he whispered.

"Brenda. She's not too bad. The one who was on last night gave me a right bollocking. She wouldn't give me a sleeping tablet. Bitch."

"Bitch. I think they want us to suffer," Cat-Hater snapped, "They all think I'm violent, I've never been violent in my life. They're trying to provoke me. If I do anything, it will be their fault. I have to fight my urges."

"Don't let them win," stressed Elaine. A young man sat in the corner, staring into oblivion. "Just because she could be a fashion model, she thinks she can treat me like shit," she continued, preoccupied by the previous evening's events. The young man spoke,

"I don't care anymore," his eyes shone as though they had been polished. "I'm out of it. I hate life. I'm not going to live anymore." He laughed at the wall. An army of ants sped across the floor. Alarmed, Cat-Hater lifted his legs off the floor. The other patients did not appear to have seen the ants. Thus, Cat-Hater re-positioned his legs and tried not to worry about why he was the only person who could see them.

The fat one opened the smoking room door and looked at Cat-Hater. He glared back and she was gone. "Shall we shut the door?" he asked. Elaine rose, immediately, and closed the door. Two minutes later the fat one returned and, wearing a perfectly perturbed expression, swung open the door. The presence of the weirdo, returning after two weeks sick leave, only worsened his situation.

"Sorry I haven't been around," she said, "you're looking much better. How're you doing?" She had cut her hair and dyed it blond.

"Fine." Fingering strands of gelled hair, she enquired if he was still writing. "If I didn't write I would go mad," he replied. He had not noticed her hair. She locked herself in a toilet and silently wept.

A new admission, a seventeen year old, named Tom, arrived on the ward with glazed eyes and was immediately treated with anti-psychotic medication. His youthfulness provoked much discussion amongst patients and staff, alike. "He shouldn't be up here. He's a kid," he heard someone say. On another occasion, he overheard a conversation between nurses who commented on the young man's lack of self-confidence. Tom, who, evidently, was unaccustomed to having his brain blown apart by legal chemicals, spent days stumbling about in an anaesthetic daze. When a week had lapsed and he was still stumbling, especially when nurses were near, Cat-Hater had begun to become suspicious.

He was saddened about being cast as a spectator in a game of life and death, in which each participant could cross the line of self-destruction at a whim. He was even more saddened that he, also, was a participant; his fate determined by the whims of a doctor. Tom had plenty of time to grow up. For Cat-Hater, swallowing his first pill, spelt pill popping perpetuity. He knew that growing was never graceful and ageing always unacceptable. He despised the ward for hastening the calling card of inevitability, the fatefulness of probability and began to sense death whispering behind his shoulder. The devil makes a mean adversary, when your back is against the wall. He would rip out cement and watch the bricks fall.

The moment Tom and the pseudo-suicidal woman met, they knew that they represented the other to their own fucked-up heads; theirs was a symbiotic relationship, based on the exchange of symptoms and sexual fluids. They swapped tips on methods of self-harm and Tom learned about the most successful techniques for achieving death. He was grateful for having experienced such a joyous initiation into the ward and soon discovered self-confidence, hitherto unknown to him. Although the merry dance that they led the nurses boosted their shrunken minds, when the nurses confiscated their shoelaces, Cat-Hater knew that their romance was doomed. The next step was to remove them from one another. Thus, the woman was discharged, whose sullen expression had been replaced by a friendly smile and dressing gown by blue eye shadow. Cat-Hater contemplated what she would do next to be reunited with the ward and her boy lover.

Meanwhile, the most repulsive man on earth, now, reigned over the ward. His pubic lice were so ubiquitous that even Cat-Hater's skin crawled. At every opportunity, Cat-Hater tried to escape to the hospital grounds for walks. He would phantasise about travelling overseas and seeing the real world. India's sun reflected, like a mirror, deep in his imaginary life. With summer near it was easy to recline on the grass and pretend that he was in Madras. He wished that he could sleep his life away, but every time he opened his eyes, he saw green walls. Even when outside the greenness, he felt shut within, like the contents of a box with no opening. Every attempt to beat his way out culminated in an injection in the arse.

One day the repulsive man came out to play. Sitting opposite him in the hospital café, Cat-Hater visualised him cutting the throat of a local vicar, who had thought exorcism would help relieve him of his daemons. The story had made the local paper. The perpetrator mistook Cat-Hater's leg tremor for a sexual advance. "You playing footsy with me?" said the human beast.

"No," spluttered Cat-Hater, in fear for his life. Having his throat cut by a psychopath would not be his chosen way out. He excused himself and left Satan to his cup of tea. Almost as repellent, was watching him flirt with a bloated corpse of a woman, who had started painting her face orange and singing love songs, with incorrect lyrics. Cat-Hater only occupied the television room when he needed a change of scenery, but, now, chose to avoid the room, whenever the aforementioned individuals were present. Mostly, however, repulsive man sat in the smoking room which, Cat-Hater, being a smoker, could not avoid. Thus, it was with some relief that Cat-Hater reacted to the news that he was to be transferred to another ward. No explanation was provided; he did not request one, in hospital, one did what one had been told.

The second ward was uncarpeted, but the staff proved to be almost welcoming. He was introduced to a kitchen in which, he was informed, he could make his own drinks. He made a coffee and tried to settle. The smoking room stank of dirty bodies; the great unwashed crouched over cigarettes and glanced, with disinterest, at their new roommate. Cat-Hater walked from wall to wall until his cup was empty and spent the rest of the day walking up and down the ward.

The following day a nurse told him that a group discussion was about to take place. Deducing from her tone of voice that his presence was not optional, he agreed to participate. He joined the circle of chaotic minds and thought he would explode, if compelled to lie about the content of his thoughts and feelings about the hospital and all within her. A tall, dark haired man stood over the throng, like a messiah surveying his sheep. Looking intensely through his horn rimmed spectacles; he announced his status, a doctor, his steady European voice rolling out his name, "Marco."

Marco was the kind of twat who emanated empathy so considered, so precisely congruent, that he should have been a first class, third class, person centred counsellor, not a psychiatrist. His words, like his existence, were measured. He began the discussion by asking everyone to introduce him or herself. When it was Cat-Hater's turn, he winced in his seat, his twisted torso reflecting the twisted words outside his head. He had realised that Jude was the name on his birth certificate, the label of reference prescribed to him by the hospital staff. Before he announced his name, he felt a unanimous pause of expectation, followed by a wave of relief, when, even surprising himself, he enunciated the name, "Jude."

"How long have you been in hospital, Jude?" asked Dr. Marco.

"A couple of months, I think." It felt more like years. A young person who, the previous evening, had been admitted barefoot, stated his name and said that he had been in hospital for twenty-five years. Cat-Hater guessed that he was twenty-five years old. Marco asked the patients if they ever felt threatened by other patients.

"Sometimes, when people are really bad with their illnesses, I do," answered a polite, older woman. She presented no obvious signs of distress, but Cat-Hater Knowing that whilst judgements were unacceptable, assumptions were unavoidable, assumed her appropriate interactions to be masking her true state of mental chaos.

A young woman lapping up the doctor's question like a hungry cat meowed, "I'm more scared of what I might do, than what the other patients could do to me." Cat-Hater nodded, in silent approval. She had spirit, he would watch his back. Afterwards, the occupational therapist congratulated him on doing well in the group; her mouth resembled that of a frog and broke into a smile. At that moment, Cat-Hater despised himself, perhaps, more than he had ever done. He had buried his instincts, like rubble, beneath a mound of appropriateness. He had become a good boy, a faithful hound, obeying every command in exchange for a stroke. A tear struck his cheek, building into a fountain, which spluttered out of the wall and stained his knee with invisible water. He touched his knee, but felt only the dry rot of muscles, which had been overstretched, in the simple act of pacing. Mystified by the experience, he retired to his bed. Flowing water bled down his face. He descended into the flow and alone in the world, transferred his feelings onto a pillow.

A nursing assistant poked her head around the curtains surrounding Cat-Hater's bed. She enquired about his health. "I wish I was dead," he sobbed. She claimed that she would ask a nurse to talk to him. He awaited the nurse, practising, in his head, a monologue, until he was word perfect. "I will walk until my feet run red; my mind devouring thoughts, until my thoughts drop dead. I shall walk until I am dead." A nurse did not come;

Cat-Hater vacated his bed and walked.

Later that week, Brotherlylove visited. He arrived bearing his favourite frown of indifference and twelve cans of Pepsi Max, donated by his Mother, which he had requested a week ago. "Mother asked me to come, she needed a day off," he began. "You're lucky to have visitors. I bet most of these have no one. Probably, abandoned by their families."

"Shall we go down to the café?" Suggested Cat-Hater.

"Mother said you were allowed off the ward. I'm not thirsty, let's stay up here." Brotherlylove's eyes wandered all over the ward and digested the visible idiosyncrasies of the other patients. Cat-Hater was ashamed of his brother's malevolent eyes. "He's a bad case," he whispered to Cat-Hater, observing no shoes man climb along the corridor. "If he had a Mother like yours, he'd have a pair of slippers."

"Perhaps, you could buy him some slippers and bring them in, next time you visit." Horrified, Brotherlylove changed the subject.

"Well, the medication must be suiting you. The last time I saw you, you were away with the fairies. I'm not used to having a sensible conversation with you. Stay on it, this time. I'm not going through that again. Do you remember what you were like? Bleeding and everything." Cat-Hater bit his lip so hard, that he thought he would bleed again.

"It's a shame that the nurses, up here, don't wear uniforms."

"I suppose, if they did, we would know that they weren't patients," quipped Cat-Hater. When his brother had left, Cat-Hater raged at the walls. He decided that he, too, would leave and leapt out of the door, followed by a couple of nurses and a nursing assistant. He did not fight them; rather, when they grabbed his arm, he let it become limp and walked back onto the ward. One of the nurses said that she would like him to see a doctor, who was currently on the ward. Subsequently, he cursed himself for exhibiting a lack of self-control and his medication was increased. For the expression of emotion, he had been punished. His only excuse for permitting it, the seductive power of the doctor's appealing eyes and smooth bedside manner.

Cat-Hater sucked on his roll-up as though it were a toxic lollypop and looked out at a nubile form, so angelic, that it could not possibly have been real. For before him stood a noble youth, whose physical beauty corresponded to that of Cat-Hater's psyche. "Can I nick a light? Smiled the youth. "I'm Aliester."

Louise M. Hart

CHAPTER TEN

I see love in the expression of his eyes; his failure to acknowledge my new hairstyle was definitely a sign. His mental health is improving and he will soon be as well as me. My heart shattered, when they moved him from the ward. It is time that I played my trump card and moved, also. Everyone knows about Richard and Bill; I shall tell the others that working with my husband's fuck buddy is making me ill.

Bill is practising avoidance by being rotared on different shifts from me. I am happily indifferent. For my marriage broke, not when he fucked my husband up the arse, but when Richard said his vows, without emitting a laugh. I laugh a lot, now. I am free to do what ever I want. I can gobble the paperboy and take the doctors out to lunch. So, why have I not? Is something wrong with me? All I think about is Jude and imagine what he wants to do to me.

Jude makes life interesting. Without his existence, the human race would be as dull as clay. And my days would comprise only work, with no opportunity for mental play. In this universe, there is no meaning beyond Jude. In my imagination, like a Botticelli nude, he exemplifies truth to non-believers, amongst whom I used to count myself.

Now, my mission is to move from poverty of ideas to poetic wealth. I perceive him as he, really, is; not a mixed-up kid, who has smoked too many spliffs, but a guardian of life, who has been denied the right to live.

When I do not think about Jude, I ruminate about myself. The pneumatic drill in my skull draws me into submission. His beauty makes darkness shout out in despair. He radiates the light, which fills my heart with love and care. He is like a lover of old, whose existence was foretold in romantic novels, which I have never read. He is my ancient mariner, lost at sea, who, when discovered, will sleep beside me. I dream about him day and night; our plights, intertwined by mental flight, are one and the same. When he ceases to fight, he will be well again, with a good woman by his side.

My belly aches with unrequited love and reminds me how good I am, for making a living pretending to be giving, when I am rotting to the core. I used to be a slut of the ward. Now, I have the horn for only one. And, thus, my stomach roars to avenge this whore for wanting to be more than a nurse to the terminally wasted. I would rather drink claret than suck student nurses, Antacids are a poor substitute.

I have never read Shakespeare or an original text by Freud. Does that make me stupid, or not easily fooled by the will to pretension? I have never travelled beyond Paris or eaten Thai food. Does that make me tasteless or authentic? I have never been bullied or burgled or buggered against my volition. I am a walking apparition of all that is stable and solid and secure. I know that I am okay. It is not that I am stupid, I am, just, not that bright.

Where does brightness lead? Admissions to ward D3, mental exhaustion and unfulfilled needs. My own needs are gratified in the form of dreams soon to be realised. In contrast, Richard is beyond hope, transforming our house into a shag pad is the only way he can cope with loneliness. His twice nightly will shortly become twice a year. I hope that I never see him again.

My interior life is the lucid type; I know about these things. How can I want revenge, when I still wear my wedding ring? Regarding Bill, I desire to see him swing. Chop off the head of the sodomite who penetrated the heart of my life and watched it bleed. Richard was merely a pawn, a pathetic piece on a chessboard. I was the Queen, who took him, myself, many times and thrust until he screamed. Why must I always be an other, daughter, nurse or wife? Identity is meaningless, when you have to think about others before opening your mouth.

As for those who cut their wrists in order to be freed on a hospital ward, where our attention becomes a kind of reward I refuse to inflate their egos. You see, I have got a cause.

Jude defies categorisation. Without his chemical

imbalance, he would be a hero of our nation. I am just ordinary, pretending to be extraordinary, pretending to be me. I hope that he takes his medication when discharged, only then, will he be functional and do as he is told. This mental illness is too big for me, were it not for Jude's presence I would get a job in a factory.

If they were all to take their pills, I would have no job making me ill, no patients trying my patience; I would live my life in the throes of ecstasy. The release of pressure, like the withdrawal of a knife, would expose my being to the breadth of life.

When I was born, my parents mourned the death of their liberty. I was an unwanted gift, which they could not give away, until I was old enough to live independently. Perhaps, if I had I been a boy, I would have generated some joy. But, I was, rather, a girl without a curl in my hair, and a shout in my throat.

Oh Daddy, you did me wrong. You taught me not to cry. For this, I curse you. I was your child and you hurt me. Penny chews and lollypops never cured a broken spirit. I remember how you sat in your chair, unaware of my suffering. I tried to tell you, but you would not listen. My voice built into a screech, until finally, tears appeared. I saw you retch, believing me to be attention seeking. I was not seeking attention I was seeking you. Oh Daddy, I miss you. And Richard, too.

CHAPTER ELEVEN

Framed in the doorway, Aliester slid his lips around his roll-up. He perched an arm against the wall and adapted to his surroundings, like a lizard to the desert. Cat-Hater inhaled nervously, each puff a race to be won before it had begun. The urge to speak to the languorous stranger burned his throat, his mind rendered blank with superfluity. He squeezed his grey matter between his fingers and tried to access wondrous words which, he knew, were buried like rusty pennies at the bottom of the wishing well of his consciousness. Aliester spoke first. "Are you bipolar?

"I used to be a schizophrenic," Cat-Hater replied, "then, I got better."

"I killed a cat, so they put me in here," Aliester continued, "I was only trying to prove the theory that cats have nine lives. The problem was that, after I had stabbed it eight times, it got angry and shat on my shoe, so I threw it out of the window. One of the neighbours saw and phoned the police. I'm lucky, I could have been charged." A wave of shock swept over Cat-Hater. Aliester rolled his shoulders and walked off.

After leaving the smoking room, Cat-Hater peeped

into the TV room, where he saw Aliester languishing on a chair. Before the other man could observe him, he advanced to the dormitory, passing two nurses. "The weight's falling off him."

"He's a gay boy, you know." The emotional pain, which only arises from hearing a truth, which should never be heard, tore at his heart, like a knife into flesh. He wanted to grab the nurses' necks, to reduce them to the rubble they really were, to listen to their final breaths. Rather, he forced himself to walk on and stage a show of indifference. Nevertheless, he hurt, to the pinnacle where hurting felt good. Cat-Hater drew the curtains around his bed. He placed his hands beneath his T-shirt and plunged his grubby fingers into his rib cage. Someone had entered the dormitory. Cat-Hater heard the sound of tuneful whistling. He recognised the tune as a song by The Beatles and strode out to see who was whistling it. Aliester stood erect, "Do you know Sexy Sadie?"

"Yeah, it's by The Beatles," Cat-Hater enthused, "it's on The White Album."

"The greatest album ever made." Then he was gone. Cat-Hater strained his ears until the whistling faded, Aliester's absence leaving a vacuum filled with the scent of cheap body spray. Cat-Hater sniffed the air; his stance addressed the spot were the other man had stood. Beside Aliester, Cat-Hater had felt frail and insignificant, like a cobweb on the foot of Michelangelo's David.

He rubbed his stomach, which had become as hollow as his cheeks; his jeans drooped beneath his crotch and gathered below his knees. He decided that he would eat more. Better a medication paunch, than the look of a starving refugee.

When teatime meds were dispensed, Cat-Hater stood near the medication trolley waiting for his name to be called. Behind it, the radio in the smoking room vomited DJ talk. Cat-Hater tried to drown out the drivel by listening to his thoughts, but when a nurse called him, he heard the DJ mention schizophrenia. He refused to take his tablets and marched down the corridor.

In the evening, he forced himself to speak, breaking through the audible barrier of silence in the smoking room. The voices of his heart rebounded off the mouths of his fellow inmates, whose institutionalisation was not an affectation of themselves, but a reflection of a system, which bound and gagged their minds. He could help himself and be free of the fallacy of psychiatry, which did not even know itself. He spoke to the words behind the words; the alternate universe in which language was the truth on which all consciousness was built. He knew that the other patients resided in the same locality, for they responded appropriately in all the inappropriate places. His was the confusion of belonging, belonging to that which was inaccessible to the mass. Although, he could move in and out of two realms, he found it difficult to return. Were the alternate to seize control, would he remain forever a patient in this shit hole? If palpability won him over would he become a faceless slave of homogeneity, a factor of the life experience with its pretence of fact?

Che only visited Cat-Hater once more. He arrived on the ward like a dog released from his leash ready to defend his comrade against the nurses' attacks. His comradely concern, concerned Cat-Hater who, in a sudden flash of inspiration, realised that Che's interest in him was not even partly sexual, but wholly political; the party could not afford to lose one of its staunchest defenders and the ten pounds a month he contributed to party funds. He decided to defend himself.

Che's new haircut offended Cat-Hater to the extent that a single glimpse of it terminated his desire for the now short and spiky friend he had hitherto masturbated over in the secrecy of his own bed. He pretended not to notice Che's hair and proceeded to stare at the floor, where he could escape from his disgust. "How are you?" Enquired Che. Cat-Hater had grown to despise this question more than any other.

"Fine." He could hear the irritation in his voice and knew that Che would, also.

"Are the nurses being okay, now?" Che hesitated, "you said that the ones on the other ward were a load of bitches."

"They aren't too bad."

"There is another demo on Saturday. Things are really kicking off. It's a shame that you're in here, I know how much you love demos." It was true; Cat-Hater had been an untiring veteran of countless demonstrations. Now, he was immersed in dreary silence. "I think I was at the first one you went to. Do you remember when I had to stop you goading that copper? I knew then, that you'd never lose your fire for politics." Cat-Hater had lost his politics when he decided that dictatorship, whether of the proletariat or the bourgeoisie, was only the veneer in the expression of the meaning of himself. His fire continued to burn for himself. His struggle to overthrow the social order had become a struggle; the ruling class replaced by psychiatrists, the agents of the state by nurses, the proletariat was him, of course.

"I've brought you a paper. There's an excellent article in it about globalisation." Cat-Hater glanced at the familiar red lettering on the front of the socialist newspaper.

"It's okay. I don't want it." He said, lowering the tone of his voice in an attempt to soften the blow. Stunned silence. He could hear Che's thoughts reeling like an engine, "I haven't read it for months."

"That's alright, let me know when you feel ready to read it again and I'll bring it in."

"I'm not interested anymore."

"That's because you aren't yourself at the moment. When you're feeling better, you will be interested. You are bigger than this system."

"I know that." Cat-Hater knew that the system to which he referred was different from the one to which Che alluded. "I don't want to be in the Party anymore." The moment lingered beyond reproach; Che was too wise to employ his powers of persuasion on a poor, disempowered comrade who was too ill to know his own mind.

"Shall I visit you, next week?" He asked.

"I don't think it's a good idea. I know my mind better, now, than I ever have. Will you tell the other comrades that I don't want to be contacted?" Cat-Hater raised his head and watched his former friend leave the ward. Che did not turn around and see the lines of anxiety rush across Cat-Hater's brow or the way he pulled his hair, which had grown almost to the length of his own.

"Traitor," snapped a nurse as Cat-Hater walked by. He turned and looked into the dark recesses of the nurse's heart. The nurse registered only puzzlement. Not only were the nurses omniscient, but they had sonic hearing.

Aliester strolling down the corridor on a warm, summer day. His shoulders were broad enough to hold the weight of an ego, which Cat-Hater knew, would never crumble beneath the load of legal drug addiction. His hair promised to shift his neck in Cat-Hater's direction, exposing hints of flesh beneath its fair strands. Every detail of his physical form suggested grandiosity of design; only his shuffle betrayed his status. Sunlight illuminated his path.

The distillation of time in a moment, a being made real by feelings, which gathered around Cat-Hater, like trees in a fecund forest. He did not want to reduce Aliester to a seduction technique; but to possess him, to lie within his bones, to drink the skeletal fluid of his loins. He did not want to seduce him; he would not lie to his heart, he wanted Aliester to seduce him. His eyes refused to look beyond the walls of the smoking room. His legs rejected the urge to walk into the corridor.

He fought to reassemble his thoughts and grabbed the novel, he was currently reading. A woman sitting in the corner of the room regarded Cat-Hater with a smile. "You're always doing something," she said, "reading or writing, or drawing. I can't read anymore." An undergraduate who was recovering from her third relapse since starting university, her dull eyes stared out behind oval glasses as though pleading for help.

"Why don't you start slowly, just a paragraph a day and then, build it up gradually." Had she called him a spy, or had he imagined it? Paralysed with anxiety, he was unable to vacate the room until she had left. He fell onto his bed and ruminated.

Had his subconscious manufactured a portrayal of someone who was mentally unwell? Was he merely an actor on a stage, where presentation was the measure of one's worth? Maybe, he proved that Thanatos worked. Alternatively, perhaps, everyone, including Aliester, thought him a spy.

Aliester sat in the TV room talking to a nurse. Because the television had been turned off, Cat-Hater felt safe to enter. He picked up a magazine and discreetly perched on a chair near enough to eavesdrop on the conversation. "Why won't you sign it?" He heard Aliester plead. "Don't you believe in righting injustice?"

"He murdered people," replied the nurse.

"He was a scapegoat, like all my family; my Dad the Ripper, my Mum Myra Hindley. Do you think she really killed those kids? I know that she didn't, because she told me. A Mother would never lie to her son, would she?

"I'm afraid I have to take those petitions off you." The nurse oozed composure. Aliester handed her some pieces of paper, stood and left the room, without even glancing at Cat-Hater.

Cat-Hater rolled a cigarette and headed towards the smoking room. Upon entering, the female student greeted him with a smile, which seemed to stretch the entire length of the room. "As soon as I saw you, I knew we had a spiritual relationship," she said. He attempted to return the smile; she was, after all, genuinely ill. Still shaking, due to the conversation he had overheard, he transferred his anxieties into a discussion about the, "fog," between men and women.

Nurse Parry hovered outside the room, having successfully manoeuvred a transfer to Cat-Hater's present ward. She knew that he would be pleased to see her again. However, when she saw her angel talking to another woman, and one who was marginally more attractive than she was, her heart tipped. When she said hello, he did look up and her subsequent attempt to explain that she had been transferred to the present ward, was greeted by a mere, "I thought you worked on this ward, anyway." She concluded that the presence of the other woman had necessitated him to cover his enthusiasm. Her imminent priority was to ensure the quick discharge of the grey Madonna, whose tits were smaller than her own. Nurse Parry's scramble to sit beside Cat-Hater coincided with Aliester's entrance into the room, where, once again, he stood, framed like a fine oil painting.

"So how's things?" She asked Cat-Hater, her words, carried away like dust in the air, elicited no response. Nurse Parry left Cat-Hater to engage with his presumed hallucinations and embarked on her nursely duties.

The only hallucination with which Cat-Hater had been engaged was the figure of Aliester, who stood before him as solid as a brick. Spex, as Cat-

Hater had christened the student, continued to dribble words. Cat-Hater and Aliester communicated in silence.

He looked from Aleister to Spex, two different consciousnesses in two different wrappings. It was sex, which differentiated them, which polarised their compositions, which dictated his reaction to whom they had learned to become. If he could subtract their sex from their identities, his reaction to one would be his reaction to both. But, he could not take away their sex. He glanced into Spex's eyes and saw a forbidden smile, reserved for him, alone. He liked her and, after all, maybe it would divert the nurses from the true scent of his desires.

Aliester followed Cat-Hater out of the room. "Boys like you will never be wallflowers," he throbbed.

"Oh. I dunno, you would be surprised," Cat-Hater replied, regretting his coyness, the second it was revealed. Without warning, he felt his left buttock being crushed between hungry fingers.

"Sexy Sadie," whispered Aliester into his friend's ear. Then he was gone.

CHAPTER TWELVE

"You like it up the arse, cock sucker." They were teasing him, fucking with his mind. Cat-Hater knew that had he been paranoid, he would have punched into oblivion every nurse who thought he or she understood the nature of his sexual proclivities. The culprit, whose mouth had voiced these profanities, sat immediately outside the smoking room laughing with a colleague. How could they laugh, when all around were dying?

He darted from the room, hoping to eschew the barrage of insults, which followed him every time his mind dared to express a sexual thought. But, he had not been quick enough. This time they clung to the air, like billowing smoke and followed his trajectory to his bed area. "Give it to him, pervert."

"Arse fucker."

"You're no man. You're a pussy in trousers."

"Fuck him 'til it hurts."

His conscience adopted multitudinous voices, each one different in tone and inflection. They reached out to Cat-Hater like flowers disembodied by the wind; petals torn and roots straining from the ground, but these flowers were not the pretty inspiration of poetic verse. Rather, each possessed thorns, which jabbed at his psyche and bled dry his brain.

Cat-Hater tried to crush then between his ears, but even the sound of music played on his ipod would not deaden their vengeful impact. The curses of the nurses were his own, his doubts and fears externalised in alien forms. The aliens surrounded him. But, he was not made to be a space cadet. He was a space with form.

Spex became Cat-Hater's protector; whenever Aliester invited him to accompany him to the hospital café, he would wrap her around him, like an iron robe, prohibiting the touch of all others.

Saved by pure woman. I am less than she, for whilst trying to impress her with my erudition, I, really, only think of he whose presence manipulates my mind. She only thinks of me. I have disowned my sense of honesty and am, but, a villain, dressed as a saviour. I have become the bad boy I have always wanted to be.

"Have you heard of Charles Manson?" Asked the hinged mouth beneath the cut glass eyes of Aliester. Both Cat-Hater and Spex answered affirmatively. "Will you sign my petition to get him freed?" Aliester produced from his pocket two pieces of folded paper, which he laid on the table before his friends.

"He's a murderer," pleaded Spex, "if they let him

out he'd be a danger to society."

"Society!" Aliester laughed. Cat-Hater knew that it was society, which had secured their hospitalisation. "Don't you think society gets things wrong? Prisons are full of innocent people," continued Aliester.

"I know that, but Charles Manson was guilty."

"Like the Guildford Four?" Snapped Aliester. Polarised from the inside out, Cat-Hater sat in silence. Once so decisive, each viewpoint, now, represented another of equal worth. His silence was pretence for securing objectivity; he followed every bend and curve of the ensuing debate.

"Alright then, I'll sign it," conceded Spex. Aliester thrust his shoulders back and expanded his chest like a peacock before a hen.

"I know that you will sign it, Jude," he said. Looking at the petition, Cat-Hater noted that Spex had neglected to write her address. He signed his name as illegibly as he could and handed it back to Aliester. "I want to get a thousand signatures. Will you guys help me? We could start in here."

"The nurses will go ape," giggled Spex.

"We can avoid them," Aliester pulled out some more petitions and handed one to Cat-Hater and two to Spex, who, proceeded to claim that she would obtain more signatures than either of the men. Cat-Hater watched her scramble over the tables and knew that, to Aliester, every signature obtained by him would be worth at least five elicited by Spex. He felt like a musketeer on a furtive mission to defend his prince. Like being catapulted back to the times when he had stood outside shops and factories yielding people to sign petitions as a premise to sell them a socialist newspaper, adrenaline flooded his stomach. Would he be shouted at, abused, even ridiculed? He was fearful, but, fear was an emotion; emotions were good. The five signatures he obtained were like five gold stars, which shimmered, in his internal vision.

When a nurse, whom Cat-Hater recognised as the woman who had taken Aliester's petition in the TV room, appeared in the café, Aliester rounded up his posse and they all headed back to the ward. He rewarded Cat-Hater's stirring work with a discerning smile and remained non-committal, when asked if he had accumulated more signatures than Spex.

Nurse Parry noticed how little time her twilight sun had, recently, spent on the ward. Without his illumination, she had the look of a rainy day; her smiles drowning like pavement beneath clouds of grey. To reclaim her smile, she plotted the downfall of an adversary so malevolent that psychosis had determined the last two years of her life. What could be more justifiable than hastening the discharge of a patient who should never have been hospitalised?

Thus, following the next ward round, Spex bounded up to Cat-Hater with the enthusiasm of a playful puppy and announced that she was to be discharged three days hence. His happiness soon evaporated into envy and finally broke into fear. For, without Spex's protection, being alone with the devastating Aliester would be unavoidable.

Later that day Aliester found Cat-Hater reading a book of poetry. "What are you reading?" He asked.

"Some poetry," Cat-Hater replied curtly, fearing the edginess of his own voice. Aliester grabbed the book and teasingly, suggested that it was, perhaps, a little anti-social to read in company.

"Let's read a poem aloud, together. You read one line and I'll read the next until it's finished. You first, Jude." Cat-Hater turned to the page of his favourite poem and read aloud the first line,

"What a th-rill," his face exploded in crimson shame.

"My thumb instead of an onion," continued Aliester. When they had read the poem, Aliester looked into Cat-Hater's eyes and suggested, "you've got issues, as they say, with women, haven't you Jude?"

Later, when Mother visited, her demeanour corresponded to that of Spex, earlier in the day. "I've just been speaking to a nurse," she enthused, "he says you're doing really well. You should be taken off your section soon." Cat-Hater felt like a schoolboy who had been awarded a prize for story writing. His story was to be the factual kind based on a fictitious life. He decided that if the doctor were reviewing his section, he should try to comply with the rules of wellness, thus, he constructed a plan to prove that he had been reborn in a shell of normality.

The television, which transmitted electrical warnings to his brain, would be his first frontier of conquest. He sat before its odious visions as though hooked to the content of the programmes it transmitted. After ten minutes, his brain became so wired, so fried, like eggs and bacon that he had to leave the room. He was surprised that he could walk away without breaking into a sweat soaked run. He would reconstruct himself and, in turn, mould reality into that which he would become.

The day of Spex's departure was a day of joyous loss. The unambiguous regard in which he held Spex, whose sweet like doughnuts character, contrasted sharply with Aliester's hidden depths, was antithetical to the ambiguity of emotion he felt towards Aliester. Cat-Hater knew that had been able to change his mindset, he would have claimed her for a bride. Rather, he spent his waking seconds dreaming of a world in which he could guiltlessly partake of an appetite, which he had forbidden.

Spex sat beside Cat-Hare waiting for her

medication to arrive. Once she had grabbed the clear bags of lethal pills, she would be free to leave the hospital. He watched her twist her fingers into shapes, which, even he could not have made. Her head downcast, she looked like a prisoner before a closed gate. She was an angel, whose goodness had been punished by fate. He wished that he could have embraced her, telling her that everything would be okay, but he knew that it would not and could not lie without crossing himself. He was not even Catholic and touching another human would have hurt him to the bones.

"They always leave people waiting for hours for their medication," said Cat-Hater, "they do it deliberately, to see how we'll react." Spex was too absorbed in the horror of waiting to react to Cat-Hater, her cats cradle fingers screeching out in pain. "It doesn't take this long for a fucking pharmacist to make up a prescription," he added, inhaling his friend's anxiety, like poison. Nearly four hours later, a nurse handed Spex her medication. She took it without raising her head. Cat-Hater overheard the nurse say that she hoped that she would never see her in hospital again and knew, from his own experiences, that this meant that she expected her imminent return.

Spex walked over to Cat-Hater and said that she would like to give him her phone number. "Write it in here," he said, opening the book he had been reading, the Collected Poems of Sylvia Plath. Inside the cover, for posterity, she shakily inscribed the digits of her phone number. "I'm not on the phone," he responded. When she was out of sight of the ward, he crossed himself and even whispered a secret Hail Mary.

Spex had left and the world was both dark and light. Its opulence offered Cat-Hater transient moments of insight into secrets held beyond thought and vision. He reached into hidden corners of his mind and dusted away cobwebs blurring his view. Like the world, he was both old and new. His fears were universal; the whole system was inverted. He was a mere reflection, an echo of perversion. His punishment for lustful thoughts could not have been more pervasive than it had become. He would transform the shouting in his head into screams of fun.

Being alone with Aliester proved to be more ecstatic and less torturous than Cat-Hater had expected. Daily visits to the café provided brief glimpses into his friend's twisted psyche. He spoke of his belief in Satanism and his communion with Charles Manson, sometimes, even pausing mid-sentence to allow Charlie to come through. Cat-Hater enjoyed playing with the devil. Only, later, in his bed, did he question his own morality and conclude that he had killed God in his own head.

A sunny afternoon in July. Aliester approached from behind. He had a surprise for Cat-Hater, something to enhance his mind. Our fair heroes headed for the secluded ground behind the hospital. Aliester fingered the resin like an expectant virgin; Cat-Hater counted his breaths in anticipation. "It's been so long," he cried. The spliff was loaded like a gun. Cat-Hater inhaled so deeply that he nearly drowned. Aliester led him on a drug induced ride in which he chose to dismiss all his sorrows and make each second a record to add to his script. By stripping his soul, he had become equipped to face tomorrow with a knowing smile. He would spend his life beside great Lucifer's child.

When Cat-Hater and Aliester had shared two spliffs, they walked to the front of the hospital and reclined on the sun soaked grass. It was the kind of day when kids stripped in gardens and adults made love to soil with garden tools. Cat-Hater and Aliester looked to heaven and saw shapes unfold. "Listen to the clouds," said Cat-Hater. "Can you hear them breathe?"

"Breathe! Breathe! It's Charlie," his friend replied.

"Is he happy?" Cat-Hater asked. Aliester rolled onto his side and looking into Cat-Hater's eyes, whispered.

"You have opened my heart shaped box." Cat-Hater returned Aliester's look and saw no longer a devil, but a messenger from above, someone born to teach him to love.

"Nirvana."

Nurse Parry clasped rage like an infant whose dummy had been taken from her. Perhaps, he, really, was gay. He seemed more than a little taken with Aliester, that psycho case, who would not be discharged for a very long time. (Jude, if only you would speak to me. Your words would complete me). Even her loving glances were treated with distance. He had negated her existence and made her life a hole never to be whole again. Her loneliness had blossomed into eternity, each moment expressed by the impression of singularity she now inflicted upon the life process. For the first time in her existence, she had claimed her own distress.

On another warm afternoon Cat-Hater walked into fate, which looked back at him with the eyes of seduction and beckoned him to step further into the woods. The woods forbade the view of the hospital; operating as a cloak, they bound all travelling life in their fibre, both invisible and opaque. Cat-Hater's feet made indelible imprints, his companion merely glided upon the grass.

He knew so little about his friend. Who had made and thrown him into this vast den of thoughts forbidden by men? Who had given him these thoughts as a punishment? He had never seen him with a family visitor or a friend. Although Cat-Hater's body was awash with perspiration, his mind sweat more, for he was walking into wooded land with somebody he did not know. Aliester pointed to a decaying tree trunk. "Take a pew," he said, "I often come here to think." Cat-Hater was struck by Aliester's sense of ease. How could someone be so chilled of body and soul whose mind irradiated fire? "What do you think about?" Aliester asked, softly.

"I keep my thoughts in my head." They sat in silence. Unable to keep up with the speed of Aliester's tranquillity, Cat-Hater eventually caved in.

"When I was a kid we used to play in some woods. There was a tree stump, like this, which we thought looked like a dinosaur..." Aliester pressed a finger, gently, against Cat-Hater's lips. Aliester opened his mouth, slowly and carefully as though afraid of inflicting pain. Cat-Hater responded by offering the whole depth of his mouth and finally slid his tongue into Aliester's mouth. When Aliester's tongue touched his, Cat-Hater knew that he was no longer barren; a wound had been sewn and a distant world discovered.

Louise M. Hart

CHAPTER THIRTEEN

My head is hot with sleeplessness. For it is midnight and I cannot sleep. I look up and see a stain on the ceiling tiles. Slowly, it moves, transforming into a figure, who dances like Judas at his last supper. I have seen Judas many times before in the eyes of strangers, when greeting friends, even on the hands of people who claimed to love me. But, mostly I see him in the demeanours of the self-proclaimed healers who work in this God forsaken den of antiquity. Judas is my favourite disciple, because, like me, he could not be saved. My eyes are open, but I am, surely, asleep. For a figure creeps at the foot of my bed. He looks like no other I have ever seen either living or dead.

He clenches my hand with the force of solid air. Although I feel nothing, I squeeze back. We step out together as though in the repose of sleep. My eyes follow the nurses we pass who, engaged in a game of cards, seem oblivious to our presence. They regard me as a non-existent. Am I dead or just dead lucky to be anonymous? Perhaps, I have entered another realm one where nurses are blind of eye, not of heart. I think I am afraid. Mummy does not come to rescue me. For I am but a child lost at sea. A little boy with far to go. I hold on tight to him of air, aware that we are passing through the doors of the ward. Patients cannot leave the ward after eight, but I do not even hesitate. I do not need to scream and shout at those with keys, "let me out." For I am beyond restraint and invisible to the blinded eye. I merely laugh.

I try to speak, but am rendered mute. I do not blame the spook that clings to me. You see, the audible beat of my heart informs me that I still live. In a second, we are through the doors leading to the epicentre, the forbidden sphere of our gaol. On the fourth floor, where, formerly, no patient has stood, my soul will be transformed from wood into gold. Now, I know that I am going home. The stairs we climb are a simple flight, whose terminus, I believe, will reveal my plight. A door is opened without tapping in a code and exuding pride, I stand in a corridor comprising only a few feet, with offices and cameras everywhere in sight. The spirit releases my hand and I explore.

Behind every door, cameras are stored. Every camera an opportunity to record personal dramas as they unfold. Lives encapsulated in images everywhere I look, I realise that I have been chosen. But, thinking myself excluded from voyeuristic eyes, I walk on. Then I see a screen, on which an image is stored, a vision of an unborn. Although its features are indiscernible, I recognise myself. I stare at my kicking legs and sigh at the sight of my clenched fist. I was blessed with anger, even before I was sentenced to live.

The palms of my hands ache with the strain of watching the beginning of my own pain. I lift them slowly and see red. Red is the colour of the substance he shed to bare me dead before I lived. If this moment is existence, then I own it.

I have no skin I am skinless within. The pain of life is too much for I who am made of dust. And my bones are made of ice. I bleed, like Christ, translucent blood. If only the good die young, then why am I still alive? What went wrong? I am doomed mortality long to lie about wanting to die. When all I really desire is strength of mind.

The camera opens up a view of a boy of five years old. He clings to his Mother's skirt and retains his tears as though afraid to exhibit. His Mother cries enough for both of them. She is arguing with a lesser being, my Father, who was never there. My palms bleed again, minute waterfalls hitting the floor. I would wipe away the blood, if I could see it.

If death were rain, it would weep on me. If death were sea, it would follow me. If death were doves, they would swoon to me. If death were true, it would set me free. Death and the rain and the sea. And the doves.

When the camera changes frame I am back at school, blaming the other students for my hurt. They surround me like a pack of wolves, desperate for blood and my assistance with their homework. Today, my teeth are sharper than their own and they have no hospital beds to call home.

I swear revenge on those who laughed at my underwear and called me queer. I swear revenge on those who made me fearful of myself.

Suddenly, I see myself in my first place of work, victimised by bullies who claim that I shirk. Talking behind my back, no wonder I fell off the track. No wonder I lost my way. I, really, did deserve to pay. But, why did the talking never stop? Their voices grew so loud, that I had to find a place of rest. Hospital was the best place for someone who could not go slow. Now, here I stand before a life. I do not cry. I do not shout. Like a viewer, who dumbly, does not know, I stand back and watch the show.

Aliester and I eating one another's lips. I see his face and almost rip my heart out of my chest. And still, my palms run red. If I were a charmer with golden hair, could I render his repair? My misfortune is that the eyes, which I have been allocated, never see the ugly. Whilst, my lips are not fit to be considered by real beauty. The irony of life is that the blind often see more clearly than the sighted.

I feel a hand on my shoulder. Warmth encompasses me. Then, into my ear arises a voice without fear, without hesitation, wise, but with no vices. Every hair of my body stands on end and I bend to each mellifluous curve of the voice's intonation. The apparition enquires about of that which I dream. Though I am mute, he hears my disclosure. Thoughts zoom into my mind, each clear and spoken in rhyme.

I dream of restful sleep and pray that a thousand shadows keep me from revelation. I wash my sins in the morning dew and drink the air, as though born new to life's inebriation. I skip through streets of cobbled wire and yield to every lusty fire that licks my frozen thighs. And dancing cheek to cheek with hell, I unify my inner self with my outer shell. I dream of air, like ageing corn, sweeping against my neck unworn by the touch of another's lips; of music, like a silken cloud, passing through the hips of an aimless crowd and stirring rusted limbs to act upon forgotten whims and move.

When I dream, I slip into the womb of the night, where all pleasure is free from humanity's plight to die. Wrapping myself around the finger of passion's right hand, I am tired no more, I am hungry for more. I eschew the desire for sweet romance in favour of a pint of decadence and a slice of fruitcake.

I stare at the screen and see a vision so supreme that it could only be me. He is beautiful, who looks into my eyes. How could such perfection want to die? My heart is full of holes and my soul is black like hell. I, really, am not feeling well. But, he upon the screen is my mirror, and he looks like a winner. He looks like a lover, a good son and an honourable brother. The other me speaks in a voice mirroring my own. He tells me that it is time to recover.

He tells me not to escape, but to be. I begin to understand and see the real me. For, all wound up inside I have sought to hide and flee from the like process, we like to call reality. It is my duty to pursue my destiny, to rewrite history. I am, but a story.

I stand upright on revelation hill and Prometheus descends with flaming hair. His body is soul exemplified; he rides a chariot of silver clouds, which are broken like eyes. Around his neck, he wears a wreath of human hair, collected from dead men's chests. Dressed in perfectly pressed violets and dead charcoal leaves, his smiles permit me to breathe. Silent as silk, I hear him calling. On revelation hill, the grass has eyes and lips, which bleed like cherry wine. He holds a torch, which emits a flame, whose gangling tips shape the letters of my name. The torch burns my toes, and then the burning upwards goes. The streams of light express me in their glow; I have insight, because I know.

Before me, stand gargantuan doors, bearing the message, "Reveal your soul, if you seek the cure." Has any other human spirit lived to see this vision stretching out to me? Made from ivory and gold, the doors open. And the trees are bare from the waist down, wasting down to the ground.

My bed beckons me to sleep; it is after midnight. I look up at a stain on the ceiling tiles. I am free.

CHAPTER FOURTEEN

Nurse Parry looked at her clock; it was seven thirty and time to leave her sleep free bed. The sun poured through her bedroom window, reminding her that all was okay. Bathed in rays, she looked down at her body and realised that her decay was only on the inside. She collapsed into a carefully chosen outfit, for this was to be no ordinary day.

She overlooked breakfast and checked that her purse contained sufficient money. Anyone watching her leave her house would have noticed her how high she held her head and the skip in her step as she walked down the road. Although she had been wounded, she bore no visible markings. The last time she had caught a bus, she had journeyed to the City Centre, where she had met a friend, who for the price of a pint of shandy, had unzipped his trousers and served a starter in a game of sex. The smallest touch of her crotch and she became bigger than both of them combined. Her existence justified by a body, which spoke more eloquently than her mind. She was a corporeal Einstein who enjoyed a meaty dinner.

To commune with the common people, she decided to travel by bus to the railway station. The bus was redolent of sweat-trapped bodies, inelegantly squashed together. Her last journey had not been like this. Thus, she concluded that her neighbourhood had deteriorated in the last six months; too many asylum seekers, too many mentally ill. They call it a modern epidemic, but it had panned out well for pharmacists and kept her in work. She did not want to think about work. Today was her day of selfhood. She would not even allow herself to be irritated by the woman who sat beside her, who possessed an arse that stretched into tomorrow. Nurse Parry struggled to breathe. A man sitting near the front chatted happily amongst himself. She imagined he phone ringing, her colleagues wondering why she had not appeared at work.

Journey's end, and as she stepped off the bus the stench of human flesh was favourably replaced by the pollution of the city. Walking to the station, Nurse Parry was carried along in a cloud of light and shade. Her feet barely touched the ground, yet she was propelled onwards. For the first time in her life, her shoulders carried no tension, allowing her arms to swing freely against her body. Her eyes ingested the universe, embracing the wondrousness of selective vision. Whilst the clouds did not speak to her, she understood how they possibly might.

When she reached the station, she bought a packet of cigarettes from the station shop. Now, seemed the appropriate time to try one of those alien products on which so many of her patients had been dependant. Standing on platform one, she lit a cigarette. But, when the smoke hit her throat, she thought she would die spewing the contents of her stomach. Nevertheless, she continued to smoke, for the first time in her adult life, oblivious to the perceptions of those around her. The train to Brighton was due in four minutes.

The four minutes passed speedily. Usually, when awaiting a train, each minute seemed to last at least five. Two minutes later, the train advanced towards the platform. A miracle had occurred, a train almost on schedule. Her eyes rested on the front of the train, before which, upon the tracks, stood an image so intense in form and content that its existence could not be doubted. (Jude, who is so fair, standing small, with curls for hair). Nurse Parry stepped off the platform and into the path of the train, where she was consumed, irrevocably and eternally by the first and last vision she was ever to see.

Rachel stood on platform three. The train to Birmingham was already ten minutes late. Thinking of Seb in his bed-sit, accompanied only by his daemons, she dared not contemplate the source of the screams that she had heard rising from the other side of the station. He had grabbed her by the shoulders and shaken her as no other man had ever dared; she was a feisty, strong woman, not a fragile young girl. He had told her that he had been a soldier; a squaddie who fought for God and country. She had no God and her country was the universe. How could she support someone like him? And, yet, she could not delete the mental image of him with tears in his eyes.

Seb walked out of his kitchen and saw Rachel seated by the window.

Seb: You've come back.

Rachel: Have you ever killed? Has the stench of death ever clung to your nostrils?

Seb: I've been to Iraq, but found my own way back.

Rachel: See some real action, did you?

Seb: I could be your action man.

Rachel: You're a proper Mr Hyde.

Seb: Then, you must be Barbie.

Rachel: So why don't you go back and join your brothers in arms.

Seb: Because they wouldn't hold them anymore.

Rachel: I was born with a brain.

Seb: Who will listen on judgement day? That's what I want to know.

Rachel: Do you find me beautiful?

Seb: If you weren't a feminist, you could be Miss World.

Rachel: All dogs like a bitch.

Seb: I didn't invite you in.

Rachel: You cried like a baby when I said that I wasn't coming back.

Seb: You smile like the devil. I knew I'd get a chance to make you wet. Get on your knees and beg for it.

Rachel: I have never led you on. Let's have a cup of tea.

Seb: They said I had the finest machine in the army, me.

Rachel: I want a child, not a man, who acts like a boy.

Seb: I've got kids from here to kingdom come. Open up and I'll slip it in.

Rachel: I just want a lover who can be seen in the front of my car.

Seb: I want a whore who doesn't wear a bra.

Rachel: Do you know what should happen to people like you?

Seb: Castration?

Rachel: A month in hospital caring for the victims of war.

Seb: But, I'm a victim, too.

Rachel: Your words are like bullets.

Seb: Who is to be the judge, when the day is here?

Rachel: He who repents.

Seb: Then, pray for my redemption.

Seb picked up his gun and the sound of two shots awoke one of his neighbours, who bolted the door of his residence and telephoned the police. He feared for his safety. After all nutters, like the man who lived above him, should be locked away. Rachel stood in a queue in a shop in Birmingham. She had treated herself to a new bra.

CHAPTER FIFTEEN

Cat-Hater skipped onto a bus. Protected from the winter chill by a battered, black duffel coat, he was grateful to be on earth. He flashed his bus pass at the bus driver and sat at the back, where he could survey the other passengers. The whole of life presented on buses, that is, the whole of life who could not afford a car, the life in which he was interested. Conversations ebbed and flowed, but he dismissed every reference to himself. The world did not revolve around him.

In an hour, his community psychiatric nurse was due to visit him at home. He wondered why they were all called Jo or Sue and dressed in black. She would administer an injection in his arse to protect him from the dark, but he secretly knew that even without a depot injection, he would never again be subject to the will of daemons. He would, however, allow the nurse her moment of pleasure, as a preventative measure for stopping doctors entering his home, like vultures sniffing out prey.

When he arrived home, he unpacked his shopping and positioned every packet and tin in their specified places on the shelves. To a nurse, the condition of one's home acted as a signifier of wellness. Although Cat-Hater's home sparkled like diamonds, he wanted to see it gleam like gold. Thus, he brushed and dusted without a single thought in his mind. Except one, he was a writer whose time was soon to come.

He had completed his first novel. He was so proud, that his beauty had grown daily. Once a prince in search of a kingdom now had become a proletarian, who had discovered his niche in pen and ink. He had written his life, but he did not think. He would not tell his psychiatrist or nurse about his novel. For he knew that upon its publication, the world would be forced to listen. There would be egg on the faces of those he once feared.

Later, he would visit Aliester who lived for the moments they spent together and had become so depressed since losing his appeal against his section. Once he had thought Aliester had taught him to love. Now, he knew that love was not a skill that had to be learned, but was like a fine wine which had to remain unopened until it matured. Before his admission to hospital, Aliester had lived in a hostel, when he was discharged, he would have a proper home with Cat-Hater.

With Cat-Hater beside him, Aliester would become groom and bride. Like garden flowers, they would bloom together on a marital ride. The ride would have no end; its bends and curves would only lift them higher. Cat-Hater caressed a book, which he had bought as a present for Aliester, as though touching an object connected to him made him seem closer.

His nurse was due in twenty minutes. Cat-Hater rushed upstairs and put on a clean pair of jeans and a t-shirt. He sprayed himself with deodorant and walked into his bathroom to comb his hair. Standing above a washbasin, a mirror beckoned him to check his reflection. He looked at himself and smiled.

Lightning Source UK Ltd.
Milton Keynes UK
UKOW042251220313

208040UK00001B/9/P